W9-AZS-940

DISCARDED

DISCARDED

ALVIN HO

ALLERGIC TO DEAD BODIES, FUNERALS, AND OTHER FATAL CIRCUMSTANCES

ALVIN HO

ALLERGIC TO DEAD BODIES, FUNERALS, AND OTHER FATAL CIRCUMSTANCES

BY Lenore LOOK PICTURES BY LeUyen Pham

HOMER TOWNSHIP PUBLIC LIBRARY DIST.
14320 W. 151st Street
Homer Glen, IL 60491

schwartz & wade books · new york

This is a work of fiction. Names, characters, places, and incidents either are the product of the author's imagination or are used fictitiously. Any resemblance to actual persons, living or dead, events, or locales is entirely coincidental.

Text copyright © 2011 by Lenore Look
Jacket art and interior illustrations copyright © 2011 by LeUyen Pham

All rights reserved. Published in the United States by Schwartz & Wade Books, an imprint of Random House Children's Books, a division of Random House, Inc., New York.

Schwartz & Wade Books and the colophon are trademarks of Random House, Inc.

Visit us on the Web! www.randomhouse.com/kids

Educators and librarians, for a variety of teaching tools, visit us at www.randomhouse.com/teachers

Library of Congress Cataloging-in-Publication Data
Look, Lenore.
Alvin Ho : allergic to dead bodies, funerals, and other fatal circumstances ; / Lenore Look ; [illustrations by LeUyen Pham].—1st ed.
p.   cm.
Summary: A fearful second grader in Concord, Massachusetts, learns about death when his grandfather's best friend passes away and he offers to accompany his grandfather to the funeral.
ISBN 978-0-375-86831-3 (trade) — ISBN 978-0-375-96831-0 (glb) — ISBN 978-0-375-89882-2 (ebook)
[1. Fear—Fiction. 2. Self-confidence—Fiction. 3. Death—Fiction. 4. Grandfathers—Fiction. 5. Chinese Americans—Fiction. 6. Concord (Mass.)—Fiction.] I. Pham, LeUyen, ill. II. Title.
PZ7.L8682Akv 2011
[Fic]—dc22
2010046968

The text of this book is set in Adobe Caslon.
The illustrations were rendered in ink.
Book design by Rachael Cole

Printed in the United States of America

10 9 8 7 6 5 4 3 2 1

First Edition

Random House Children's Books supports the First Amendment and celebrates the right to read.

This book belongs to
Francisco Nahoe,
who gave me the idea and dared me to write it.
"Death . . . ," he said. "I bet your editor won't go for it."
Well, she did.
And here it is!
—L.L.

This one is for Kolbe.
—L.P.

AUTHOR'S ACKNOWLEDGMENTS

"I—smell—death. . . . I can smell somebody an' tell if they're gonna die."
—Dill, *To Kill a Mockingbird*, by Harper Lee

"The millions are awake enough for physical labor, but only one in a million is awake enough for effective intellectual exertion, only one in a hundred millions to a poetic or divine life. To be awake is to be alive. I have never yet met a man who was quite awake. How could I have looked him in the face?"
—Henry David Thoreau, *Walden,* 1854

Writing a book takes your soul. I know this because every time I finish a book, I will weep uncontrollably. It will start at my desk; then I will get up and walk through the rooms of my house, wailing and howling as if I have lost someone dear to me and I am looking for them. It is only when this happens that I know for certain that my book is finished. During the writing of this book, this strange weeping happened TWICE before

I got to the end. Each time was when Alvin nudged me awake enough to glimpse life, real life, for a brief second—and it was beautiful, so beautiful that I wept. And it was then that I realized why I weep at the end of a book. When your soul is taken, the feeling is not death, but rapture, which is a fancy word for losing your soul and having to look for it.

Thank you, thank you, thank you to all who worked on Alvin, especially Ann Kelley for her marvelous editing and LeUyen Pham for bringing Alvin to wonderful, joyful life. Thank you.

CHAPTER ONE

How to Get History Straight

call me alvin ho.

I was born scared, and I am still scared. And this is my book of scary stories. I tell the truth mostly, on account of that's what happens when you're all freaked out. You tell the truth, the whole truth and nothing but the truth, so help you God. And if you've read my other books, you know that they get scarier and scarier, which means that the book you're holding should have made you run away by the title alone.

So if you're afraid of creepy stories, you might

want to put this down and read something else, like *Charlotte's Web* or *Alice in Wonderland*, two books about *girls*. And girl stories, as everyone knows, are not nearly as terrifying as boy stories. On second thought, maybe you should read the dictionary, which isn't frightening at all . . . until you get to . . . "**abominable snowman** *n.* a large legendary manlike or apelike creature . . ." Gulp. Never mind. But if you're still reading this, don't turn the page. If you do, don't say I didn't warn you.

.●.●.

Normally, on this page, I'd tell you about all the things that scare me, such as:

Book reports.

Reading in class.

Thunder.

Lightning.

Poisoned darts.

Poisoned apples.

Fairy tales.

Vampires.

Principals.

Drowning in the bathtub.

But this is not normal. There's no time for all that.

There's not even time to tell you that I live in Concord, Massachusetts, which is hard to spell. Or that this was once a fantastic town where the American Revolutionary War began, with lots of explosions and bad language and dead bodies on all the lawns. But it's not that kind of town anymore. It's now a boring place on account of explosions and bad language have been outlawed except on Patriots' Day, which is when they try to start the American Revolutionary War all over again every year, charging and firing and cursing at one another, just like in the old days. But if you try to start a war or use a bad word any other day, you've got all sorts of trouble coming to you and none of the red bean mochi cakes that your pohpoh made. And as for dead bodies all over the place, I'll get to that soon enough.

But first I need to start with my history test. Miss P announced that we were going to have a history test in second grade very soon. This wouldn't be so frightening if I hadn't already taken the practice test, which was more than I could bear. Worse, I couldn't ask for help. I can't speak in school. I can scream my head off on the bus, but as soon as I get to school, my voice doesn't work. I'm as silent as a hard-boiled egg. This is on account of I have so-so performance anxiety disorder, which is a fancy way of saying school freaks me out.

And tests freak me out even more.

At our school, there aren't any tests in kindergarten or first grade. You just go to class and you learn something new every day. But in second grade, there are tests, which aren't about learning anything new at all, but about remembering something old, which is truly frightful on account of I can't even remember yesterday. Worse, you need to try to PASS the test, even the practice one. Maybe this wouldn't be so bad if they'd told me beforehand that I needed to pass the test, but they didn't tell me this until afterwards.

Then it was too late. Even worse, an envelope came home marked "To the Parents of Alvin Ho."

To the Parents of Alvin Ho

"You're not supposed to open that," said my brother, Calvin, throwing his backpack on the kitchen floor after school. I threw mine too. But I hung on to the envelope.

"Why not?" I said.

"Are you your own parent?" asked Calvin.

"No," I said.

"That's why," said Calvin. " 'To the Parents of' means that the letter is private and that your teacher wants to tell Mom and Dad something about you that she doesn't want you to hear."

"I knew that," I said. But I really didn't. Maybe I'd figured out some of it by myself, sort of, but I definitely couldn't say it the way Calvin could. So it was a good thing that my mom and dad were at work and GungGung was babysitting. I put the letter away.

After a few days, when it was too late to give it to the Parents of Alvin Ho without some sort of trouble, and I couldn't stand it any longer, I ripped open the letter and read it. Then I was very sorry I did. There was nothing in the letter that said anything good about me. If the Parents of Alvin Ho read it, there would be weeping (mine) and gnashing of teeth (my dad's) in Concord tonight, that's for sure.

So I pushed it, along with my test, into the garbage disposal between the fish skeleton and the coffee grounds, where it should have disappeared. But it didn't. Who would have thought that the disposal was allergic to tests and scary letters and would vomit it so that my mom could read it?

"It doesn't even look like you were ever in class!" screamed my dad when he saw the scary test and read the even scarier letter.

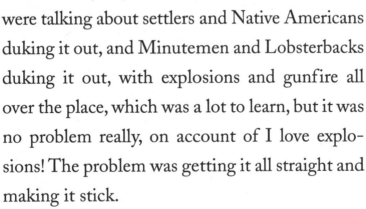

But I *was* in class. I was in class every day that they were talking about settlers and Native Americans duking it out, and Minutemen and Lobsterbacks duking it out, with explosions and gunfire all over the place, which was a lot to learn, but it was no problem really, on account of I love explosions! The problem was getting it all straight and making it stick.

"History is tricky," said Calvin when I asked him for advice on how to pass my test. It was after school and he was lying on top of his bed with his arms folded behind his head, doing nothing but looking up at the ceiling.

"The problem is that so many things have happened in history," Calvin continued.

"Yup," I said. "It's all mumbo jumbo."

"The only way to remember mumbo jumbo," said Calvin, "is to organize it."

"Organize it?" I asked.

Calvin is nine and he's really ter- rific. He's very smart and full of good advice. The only problem is get- ting it.

"What you need are pictures," said Calvin thoughtfully. "Pictures will make history stick to you like feathers to tar."

"I'm not tar," I said.

"Trust me," said Calvin. "I know from experi- ence that pictures will make anything stick, es- pecially if you draw the pictures yourself. In fact, you won't be able to delete them from your memory except with a blast of firecrackers."

"Hooray!" I yelled. "I love explosions!"

"Yippee!" cried Anibelly. She's four and she's my sister. She messes with my things, eats my food, drinks my chocolate milk and generally gets in my way. If I didn't mention earlier that she was also in my room with me and Calvin, it's on account of she's always there, like a piece of furniture. And I'd learned in writing class that you don't necessarily have to mention the furniture every time.

"Calvin wasn't talking to you," I said. "You don't even know what history is."

"But I know how to draw real good," said Anibelly.

I was this close to thumping Anibelly. But I remembered just in the nick of time the first rule of being a gentleman: No hitting, not even girls, which is really annoying. If it weren't for girls, being a gentleman would be super-duper easy.

Then Anibelly started picking up the crayons

and pieces of paper lying on the floor. "Lalalalalala," sang Anibelly. "Lalalalalala."

"*Owwwwwwwooooo,*" howled my dog, Lucy, who is also always around and likes to sing too.

"The history of Concord, as everyone knows, goes WAY back," said Calvin, going over to the table, where Anibelly was now sitting and drawing. "But you only need to remember the really important stuff."

"But that's the problem," I said. "I can't remember *any* of it."

"That's because you're trying to remember everything," said Calvin. "If you concentrate on a few major events, then it's easy."

"Like what?" I asked.

"Like the first inhabitants of Concord," said Calvin, "were the dinosaurs."

He drew a dinosaur like this:

I love dinosaurs! Mine looked like this, it's a Tuojiangosaurus:

Next, Calvin said Concord was on the landmass known as Pangaea, which started separating into different continents. So Calvin told me to draw a frying pan broken into several pieces to help me remember the first syllable of Pangaea.

After that, the Egyptian Pyramids went up.

Then the Trojan War broke out.

Then the Great Wall of China began. It looked like this:

"How come Miss P never mentioned any of this?" I asked.

"Dunno," said Calvin.

"Are you sure this is the right history?" I asked.

"History's history," said Calvin. "It's the same whether you live in Concord or in Hong Kong."

"Oh," I said.

Next, Calvin told me to draw a leaf for Leif Eriksson, a Viking dude, who was the first European to set foot on the Concord continent.

After that, Ben Franklin flew a kite.

Then a hen landed behind bars.

It was to remind me of the first syllable of Henry David Thoreau, who went to jail for opposing slavery.

After that, baseball was invented.

Then Fenway Park was built.

My pictures were super-duper!

But they were still mumbo jumbo.

And something was missing.

"Hey, how 'bout the Algonkians and Puritans?" I asked. "Miss P keeps talking about them. Didn't they have something to do with history too? Where do they fit in?"

Calvin rubbed his chin. He put on his thinking face.

"I'm pretty sure they were around before Fenway Park went up," he said thoughtfully.

"I thought so," I said. Miss P would be pleased that I knew.

But I was not pleased. I was panicked. My pile was a real mess.

"How am I going to keep 'em all straight???" I cried. "I know the dinosaurs came first, but after that . . . it's all *moong-cha-cha*!"

"It's easy," said Anibelly. "Do like me." Then she fanned out all her pictures in the right order like a deck of cards, just like that.

"Hmmm," said Calvin, looking at my mixed-up pile of pictures. "You need Plan B."

"Plan B?" I peeped. "What's Plan B?"

CHAPTER TWO

The March of History

having a girl for a sister is really annoying.

But having a brother who has a Plan B is terrific.

Calvin and I took my mumbo jumbo pictures and ran outside. Anibelly and Lucy hurried out after us. It was a bright and cool fall afternoon. The trees were as naked as skeletons, which is kind of creepy, but not as creepy as they are in the summer when they are full of leaves and dark.

Anibelly started digging holes right away with one of my carved sticks and singing at the top of her lungs. "Lalalalalalala," she sang like a little bird.

But I don't sing. I scream. *"AAAAAAAAAAAAAAACK!"*

I ran full speed ahead around the yard with my eyes squeezed shut, screaming my head off. I love digging holes too, but I love running like a maniac and exploding like a string of firecrackers even more! The only thing missing was my superhero Firecracker Man outfit; it was in the wash. Then I ran over to Calvin, who was attaching our dinosaur pictures to the side of our house with duck tape.

"It's called the March of History," said Calvin. "You march

from one event to the next. The idea is to make you *see* everything in the right order. That way you won't forget. It's like baseball—the bases are set out and there's no mistake about which way to run."

I nodded. It sounded like a great idea!

"Our house is home plate," said Calvin.

Then I followed Calvin as he marched fifty steps, which equaled fifty million years later, and we ended up in the garage, where there was a broken planter. Calvin dropped the broken pieces into the shiny black puddle on the floor that had leaked from my dad's car, and ta-da!—it was continents floating in the scary dark ocean. It was terrific!

"I'm beginning to remember stuff already!" I cried.

"That's the whole point," said Calvin.

Then we marched to the sandbox, where Anibelly helped us with the Egyptian Pyramids.

After that, we raced to the bottom of our

driveway, where our mailbox was the perfect Trojan War horse!

But the Great Wall of China was so long, Calvin said, that we would need to march into town to help us remember it.

"That's a long ways off," I said, staring down the street. "We're not supposed to go that far."

"Hmmm," said Calvin, who is always a rule-follower and not a rule-breaker, except for emergencies. "*Normally*, we're not supposed to go that far . . . but you've got history to remember, don't you?"

I nodded.

"And this is helping you, isn't it?" asked Calvin.

"Yup," I said.

"Then don't worry," said Calvin. "I'll help you cross the streets. I'm a Boy Scout."

Calvin started off toward town, and I marched right after him, turning only once to

see if Anibelly and Lucy were following. They were not. There was no sign of them. It was just me and Cal. It's hardly ever just me and Cal doing something together. It was terrific! Calvin's super-duper! He's the captain of our ship, that's for sure.

And Calvin was right. The long march into town practically tattooed the Great Wall of China to my brain where I would never forget it.

And it was a good thing Calvin's a Boy Scout. There's no sidewalk on Cambridge Turnpike on our side of the street all the way from my house to Ralph Waldo Emerson's house. Worse, I spotted the spooky Mr. Emerson on his riding mower! How Calvin got us safely to Main Street after that, I have no idea (my eyes had squeezed shut from the Emerson House on), but eventually, there we were in front of the toy shop, where Calvin always stops to look in the window.

Calvin got very, very quiet.

His breathing slowed.

His body leaned forward, like one of my carved sticks against our fence.

His eyes grew big and round.

Looking at toys in a toy shop window changes Calvin the way looking at historic battlefields changes my dad. You can tell it's still my dad, but his face is different—he looks like he's in two places at once. And Calvin looks the same way standing in front of the toy shop—his body was there, but his mind was lost.

"Wouldn't you love to have that stuffed dinosaur?" asked Calvin.

"No," I said.

"How 'bout that crane with the pulley action?" he asked.

"No," I said. But Calvin never asks if I'd like to have something he's already picked out for

himself, so I pressed my nose to the window to
see what he was looking at.

I looked to the left.

Then I looked to the right.

Then I looked straight ahead—and there it
was: Sherlock Holmes's Limited Edition Detective Kit.

My heart stopped.

My breathing stopped.

My tongue fell out.

"I'd sure love to have that detective kit," said
Calvin.

"I'd sure love to have that detective kit too," I
whispered.

"How much money have you got?" he asked.

"None," I said.

"I mean at home," said Calvin.

"A lot," I said. I had a bunch of coins and a wad of one-dollar bills rolled up inside a glass jar that used to hold nothing but organic pomegranate jam. Calvin knew it. And I knew Calvin was broke, like he always is, which is a funny way to say that his jar was empty, not broken.

"Let's go get it," said Calvin. "Then we can come back and buy the detective kit together and share it."

"No!" I said, stamping my foot on the sidewalk. "You can't stop the March of History to shop."

"No worries," said Calvin. "Shop now, march later."

Oooh, it really flipped my pancakes. That's another thing about Calvin. He's a procrastinator. The more work that needs to be done, the longer he likes to put it off. Just ask him about his science fair project.

"You can't be a detective without fingerprint dusting powder," he added. "How 'bout we go halfsies on it?"

"I don't want to be a detective," I wailed. "I JUST WANT TO SEE WHERE THE REST OF HISTORY'S GONNA BE!"

Heads turned.

A little dog on a leash sniffed my ankles.

A stroller hurried by.

"Okay, okay," said Calvin. "Quit your hollerin'." Then he taped my drawing of a leaf to a parking meter in front of the toy shop. A leaf? What did a leaf have to do with history???

After that, a fire hydrant was Ben Franklin.

Then a hen in jail got stuck to the front of a mailbox. Strange.

But Calvin was right. I could now see the right order of everything in a way that I wouldn't forget. It was terrific!

"Is this what they mean by a hysterical town center?" I asked.

"Dude," said Calvin, glancing up the street and looking very pleased. "Now you're gonna *eat* your test."

"Eat it?" I asked. "I only want to pass it."

"It's an expression," said Calvin. "It's a way of saying it'll be as easy as eating pizza."

"Mmm," I said. "I love pizza."

It was the best news I'd had all day.

CHAPTER THREE

Roofing Isn't a Hobby

when calvin and i got back to our house, the first thing I saw in our driveway was my dad's legs sticking out from under his car, Louise. If you didn't know my dad or Louise, you'd say that Louise had come sailing out of the clear blue sky and landed on top of my dad, killing him. But if you looked closely, you would see that his toes were sticking up, which meant that he was okay. He was just fixing something.

Normally, I'm so happy to see my dad home from work that I say, "Hi, Dad!" in a loud, cheerful voice and hug him like he's the best dad that ever walked into my house.

But not when he's under his car. Shakespearean mumbo jumbo was coming out from under Louise as thickly as the shiny black liquid oozing down the driveway.

"Canst thou not minister to a car diseas'd," came from underneath the car, "pluck from the carburetor a rooted sorrow?"

I think my dad was swearing at himself in Shakespeare, which is the kind of cursing they used to do in the old days when they had time to really use bad language instead of four-lettered words.

"And with some fresh oil, cleanse the stuff'd bosom of the perilous particles which weigh upon the engine?"

Silence.

Interrupting my dad when he's underneath Louise is never a good idea. It's like holding dynamite and asking for a match. So Calvin and I just stood there and listened for a while, not saying a word.

Then my dad's cell phone rang.

Clank! went something heavy.

"Owwww!" screamed my dad.

Silence.

"Hello," he mumbled, sounding annoyed.

Silence.

"What?" said my dad, still underneath Louise. "You saw my boys walking along the side of the road . . . by themselves?"

I looked at Calvin.

And Calvin looked at me.

"CAAAAAAAALVIN!" screamed my dad.

Calvin and I backed away from the car.

My dad rolled out on his creeper seat.

"WHAT'S THIS ABOUT YOU TAKING YOUR LITTLE BROTHER ALL THE WAY DOWNTOWN?"

"But—" said Calvin.

"YOU COULD HAVE GOTTEN RUN OVER!" cried my dad.

Poor Calvin.

The only time that Calvin is speechless is when he's busted.

But the good thing about getting busted with Calvin is that he's up against the flames while I only get a little warm. It's like my dad is a roaring fire and we're a couple of marshmallows on a stick, and I'm the one in the back that doesn't even turn brown, while Calvin's the one in front getting blistered.

But poor me too.

The look on my dad's face was that he was going to kill us both if it hadn't been for our next-door neighbor, Mr. Arlecchino, who appeared from his side of the driveway at that very moment. Mr. Arlecchino has perfect timing.

He always comes over just when we need him most.

"Trouble with the car again, Ho?" asked Mr. Arlecchino, giving my dad a firm handshake and a good ol' slap on the back.

"Not any more than usual," said my dad.

"Busting your boys again, Ho?" asked Mr. Arlecchino, smiling like a Buddha. He winked at me and Calvin.

"*Grrrrrrrr,*" said my dad.

I like Mr. Arlecchino. He's very funny, and he likes to give my dad lots of friendly advice, which really annoys my dad.

"If I were you I wouldn't worry about your boys," said Mr. Arlecchino, chuckling. "I'd worry about your roof."

"My roof?" asked my dad.

"It's time for a new one, isn't it, Ho?" asked Mr. Arlecchino.

"*Grrrrrr,*" said my dad.

"Can't let a roof go for too long," Mr. Arlecchino added. "No sirreee, or you'll have coons and squirrels living with you."

My dad shaded his eyes with his hand and squinted up.

"Bad weather's coming soon," said Mr. Arlecchino. "You'll be lucky if the roofers can squeeze you in."

"I'll do it myself," muttered my dad.

"Roofing isn't a hobby, Ho," said Mr. Arlecchino. "It's a dangerous job."

I looked up.

I blinked.

I could see my dad—gasp!—falling off the roof!

"Don't say I didn't warn you," said Mr. Arlecchino. "One twist of the ankle on that steep pitch and it's Do-It-Yourself Ho no more."

I gasped again.

Mr. Arlecchino turned and went back into his house.

My dad turned and crawled back under his car.

"Thou goatish crook-pated canker ratsbane" oozed out from underneath Louise. "Thine horrid image doth unfix my hair."

Mr. Arlecchino can get my dad so riled up that he'll be *moong-cha-cha,* or fuzzy in the head, for hours, even days. Sometimes my dad won't have any memory of what he was doing before Mr. Arlecchino came over, which can be very useful.

So I hurried inside.

And Calvin hurried after me.

CHAPTER FOUR

Dead Body No. 1

when you're little like me and you have an older brother that's bigger than you, you can die at any time.

Worse, it can hurt like wasabi in the eye.

"Owwwwwww," I cried. *"Owwwwooowww."*

Calvin had me in a headlock as soon as we were safely in our room. "You could have stuck up for me," he said. "I was only trying to help you with your homework."

A rubber-toy squeak came out of me.

"You just stood there like a leg of lamb!" said Calvin, who can really kick my butt.

"Alvin's gonna die!" cried Anibelly. "Alvin's gonna die!"

It was hard to tell whether Anibelly was cheering or crying for help. I couldn't see her face. The bad thing about headlocks is that you can only see your knees. Then I heard the sound of Anibelly's feet thumping quickly down the hall and down the stairs. Then I heard her no more. Whether she had gone to get help or was gone for good, I had no idea.

Lucky for me, I knew the four easy steps to escaping a headlock:

1. Rotate your body. Put your shoulder and arm against your brother's chest.
2. Put your leg behind both his legs.
3. Fall backwards and trip him over your leg.
4. Run!

If you get to step 4 and you're still staring at your knees and smelling your brother's armpit, then it's time to roll out your down-and-dirty, going-to-get-ugly Plan B.

If I had a Plan B. Calvin is the one with the Plan Bs. I only have emergency plans and survival tips—and those were in my PDK (Personal Disaster Kit), which was—cough, choke—on the kitchen floor!

I knew that Calvin knew that I knew that he

knew that I would've died right there in his armpit, if it weren't for the fact that he had a lot to do. He can never finish anything, including killing me, before he has to move on to the next thing.

"Calviiiin!" called my mom from downstairs. "Hurry, honey, or you'll be late for karaaatee!"

Clunk! Calvin dropped my head like a five-pound bowling ball. Stars scattered. Birds sang.

Then Calvin was gone, just like that.

I rubbed my head. Then I ran downstairs.

GungGung and Anibelly were playing Chinese chess in the living room. And Lucy was doing yoga ball next to them.

"May I play?" I asked.

"Hmmm," said GungGung.

"I'd really like to play," I said.

"When Anibelly and I are done," said Gung-Gung.

"Yeah, when Gung-Gung and I are done," echoed Anibelly.

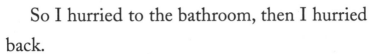

It wasn't fair. Everyone had something to do but me. I had nothing to do.

So I hurried to the bathroom, then I hurried back.

"Are you done now?" I asked.

"No," said Anibelly, sticking out her Hokey Pokey toe from underneath the chessboard.

"Where did you boys go earlier?" asked GungGung without looking up.

"Downtown," I said.

"By yourselves?"

I nodded. It was okay to tell GungGung, who never busts us. In fact, he's handy to have around whenever I'm in trouble (my mom and dad don't scream as loud). "Calvin and I did a hysterical tour," I said.

"Good," said GungGung. "Glad you boys are

interested in history. There's a lot of it here in Concord."

Silence.

"As soon as your dad comes in, I'll be leaving," said GungGung. "My friend Charlie was admitted to the hospital this morning, and I want to go see him before visiting hours are over."

Silence.

I didn't know what to say. I might soon be in the hospital too when my dad saw me and remembered our unfinished business. I wondered if GungGung would come visit *me*.

Then GungGung's phone rang.

"Hello?" he said into his phone.

Silence.

"Whaaaat?"

Silence.

"When?"

Silence.

"I don't believe it."

Long silence.

"I'm sorry," he whispered. "I'm very, very

sorry." Then he clicked off his phone and said some Chinese words.

"What's the matter, GungGung?" I asked.

"Charlie. Died."

"DIED???" I cried.

"You mean he's *dead*?" asked Anibelly, who's always interrupting our man-to-man talks.

"Of course it means he's dead," I said. "When you die, you're dead. It's over. That's it for you."

"Then what?" asked Anibelly.

"Then you go to heaven on the bus," I said. It's true. I'd seen the big bus roll into town that says "Heavenly Tours." It's mostly old people who get on and off, stopping at all the dead authors' homes in Concord to pay their last respects before going to their own final destinations.

"Isn't that right, GungGung?" I asked.

GungGung bent over the chessboard. Suddenly he looked like the burnt end of a Fourth of July sparkler, a crooked finger of ash, about to blow away. He set down the dragon piece that he

had picked up when his phone rang. He was going to use it to pounce on Anibelly's chariot, I was sure of it, but he didn't.

Instead, he hung his head.

"Are you okay, GungGung?" I asked, putting my hand on his shoulder.

"No," said my gung-gung.

His eyes closed.

He breathed in.

He breathed out.

He said nothing for a long, long time.

Finally, GungGung whispered, "I'm in shock."

I was in shock too. I'd never known anyone who had died.

"He was my best friend," said GungGung.

I nodded. Charlie was a friend to me too. His nickname was Charlie Chow Fun on account of he loved to eat chow fun, which is yummy rice noodles. I love chow fun too, and sometimes he'd call me Alvin Ho Chow Fun, which always made me laugh. And he'd always have a good word for me.

"Alvin," he would say, "you're coming along nicely."

Charlie and my gunggung liked telling stories of the old days when they were building the Great Wall of China together and fighting off barbarian invaders. After that, they stuck around for a bunch of inventions: ice cream, shadow puppets, paper, tea, kites, playing cards, dominoes, gunpowder, matches, the compass. Imagine that! Finally, when China got boring, they moved to Boston, where the excitement was just heating up.

"It seemed like it was only yesterday that we were about your age," my gunggung said. "Then suddenly we were old men. . . . It all went by so fast. We didn't even have time to say goodbye."

I stood on one foot.

Then I stood on the other.

I didn't know what to say.

Worse, I couldn't remember *what* to say. My dad had taught me and Calvin the rules of being a gentleman, and there was a rule about what to say when someone dies, but it was so creepy, I'd forgotten it.

 But Anibelly hadn't.

"I'm sorry, GungGung," said Anibelly, bending her little pipe-cleaner arms around GungGung's neck.

"Thank you, sweetheart," said GungGung, wrapping his arms around Anibelly. "I'm really sorry too."

"It must feel as bad as when my hamster died," said Anibelly. "Only bigger."

GungGung nodded. "Charlie was a big hamster, all right," he said.

Then Anibelly began to cry, not loudly like the way I do, but softly like our washing machine.

A tear rolled down GungGung's face as he squeezed Anibelly.

Then another.

And another.

I swallowed.

I breathed in.

I breathed out.

Deep breathing helps when your heart falls out of your chest. I learned this from the psycho who is my therapist, but I could never remember to do it, until now.

But I still didn't know what to say. What do you say when it feels like you've come to the end of a really great book and there's no more chapters, but you want it to go on forever?

"Maybe there'll be a sequel," I said.

GungGung's eyes popped open. "A sequel?" he asked, looking at me, puzzled.

Oops. Maybe that wasn't the right thing to say either.

"I had a funeral for my hamster," said Anibelly.

GungGung nodded. "There'll be a funeral for Charlie on Saturday," he said.

Then he sighed heavily. It was a sad, lonely sound, like the last gasp of the sun when it sets behind Walden Woods.

"I'll come with you, GungGung," I squeaked. "He was my friend too."

Gulp. Why did I say that???

But GungGung's face changed. "You would do that for me?" he asked.

I nodded, but nothing moved.

GungGung put his arm around me.

"Thank you, Alvin," he said. "Charlie would like that."

He would?

"And it would mean a lot to me," GungGung added. He squeezed my shoulder. Then he didn't say anything for another long, long time.

I didn't say anything either. I didn't know what to say. I didn't even know why I'd said what I did. The words had fallen out of my mouth before I could stop them. Go to a funeral? Isn't that the creepiest thing you could ever do?

Then GungGung took some deep breaths.

I thought he was going to pass out.

But he didn't.

Instead, he cried like a tree on a rainy night.

.●.●.

Crying is really great. Everything is always better afterwards, except when your best friend has died. Then you just cry some more. When my dad came in and saw my gunggung crying, he put his arms around him. I think it's one of the rules of being a gentleman, but I'm not sure, I couldn't remember. I was all freaked out.

By the time my mom came home with Calvin from karate, my gunggung had run out of tears. He talked to my mom for a while, then he went home.

"Alvin," said my mom. "I'm really proud of you for wanting to go to Charlie's funeral with GungGung."

"I'm very proud of you too, son," said my dad. "It takes a man to bury a man."

I said nothing. I didn't know what to say. I wasn't a man . . . and I didn't want to bury anybody.

Swoosh went Calvin's karate leg, right over the top of my head. He's always in a karate mood after lessons.

I wobbled like a bowling pin.

"Alvin's going to a funeral?" asked Calvin, turning on one foot and throwing his other leg over my head.

I wobbled again.

"Charlie died and GungGung's devastated,"

said my mom. "And Alvin offered to attend the funeral with him."

Calvin stopped. He looked at me. The look on his face said that he didn't quite believe it, but if he did believe it, he would have new respect for me.

I felt a little better.

"I'm proud of you too," said Anibelly, slapping herself across the chest with a long wooden spoon. "You never volunteer to do anything, but today you did."

Anibelly blinked.

Then she smiled.

Then she tapped me on one shoulder with her long wooden spoon. Then she tapped me on the other. This is something you do when you're especially proud of some- one; Anibelly learned it from the Queen herself on the BBC.

"Lalalalalala," Anibelly began to sing. It was time for us to help my mom with dinner. Anibelly had already laid out all the spatulas and ladles and salad tongs, and put out all the pots and pans. I liked helping too, but I could hardly move.

"As Charlie would say," my mom continued, reaching for some vegetables to chop, " 'you're coming along nicely, Alvin.' "

I smiled.

Whoooosh went Calvin's karate leg over my head. He was just jealous.

Then my dad added, "I'm sure Charlie would be proud to see you there with your gung-gung."

Proud? He's going to *see* me?

I thought he was *dead*.

Anibelly's spoon went round and round.

My dad's pots went *clang-clang-clang*.

My mom's cleaver went *chop, chop, chop.*

Calvin's karate leg went *whoosh!*

I wobbled.

The lights dimmed.

My breathing stopped.

Anibelly's singing stopped.

"Alvin?" said Anibelly. "Are you okaaay, Alvinnnn?"

It was the last thing I heard.

CHAPTER FIVE

You Can't Rub the Spot

the good news about making a Horrific Big Promise (HBP) and having everyone say how proud they are of you was that it made a greater disturbance than getting busted for walking into town by ourselves. And greater disturbances, as everyone knows, will blast away any memory of the lesser disturbance as though with dynamite!

The bad news was that it was like the other HBP (Hit By Pitch). In baseball, if you get Hit By Pitch, no matter how much it hurts, you can't rub the spot. It's one of the rules. You gotta take it like a man; there's no crying in baseball, ever.

That's also how it is when you make a Horrific Big Promise. No matter how freaked out you are by it, you can't say so, it would be like rubbing the spot.

Lucky for me, I had a chance to rub the spot without looking like I was doing it when my dad read to us from Homer's Odd Sea at bedtime. It's the true story of Odysseus going home from the Trojan War. Horrific adventures are great! Especially when they involve spies and pirates and Lotus Eaters, whatever they are. Plus they

make you want to tell your dad just how frightful your own day has been and get it over with.

But before I could get the words out, he turned to me and said, "Son, you were a real hero today."

I love it when he calls me that. Son. I love it more than my own name. And hero? My dad had never called me a hero before in my entire life.

Anibelly nodded.

Even Calvin looked at me differently.

"A hero?" I asked. "But I didn't save anyone."

"You don't have to save someone," said my dad. "Mostly, a hero knows what the right thing to do is, and does it. No hesitation. And no calling any attention to himself."

I thought about it. My dad is like that. He always knows what's right and he does it. And most of the time, you'd never even know he'd done it.

"You're a hero, Dad," I said.

My dad smiled. "Thank you, Alvin," he said. "I hope that I am."

I nodded. I liked being a hero, just like my dad.

But after that, I couldn't let him know how really freaked out I was, like I normally do, could I?

No, I couldn't.

"Good night, boys," said my dad, turning off the light.

Then the door shut, *click*. And my dad and Anibelly were gone.

Suddenly, it was as silent as the grave in my room.

And just as dark too.

"Calvin?" I peeped.

Silence.

Usually this is the time when I ask Calvin for advice and favors, on account of Calvin's pretty agreeable when he's falling asleep, not like he is during the day when he's wide-awake.

"Cal?" I tried again.

"Go to sleep," said Calvin, turning over in his bed.

"Why did Charlie die?" I asked.

"You're asking me? You're the one who was here when GungGung got the news."

"GungGung didn't tell me," I said. "And you know everything."

Calvin sighed. He rolled over.

"People die when they get to be that age," he said.

"What age?" I asked.

"GungGung's age," said Calvin.

GUNGGUNG'S AGE???!!!

I sat up.

"Does that mean—GULP—
GungGung's gonna die soon too?"
I asked.

Silence.

"Cal?"

"ZZZZZzzzzzzzzzzzzzzzz."

The problem with talking
to Calvin at this time is that
he can fall asleep just like that.
He's like a video game that
switches off by itself. But I am not. I'm afraid of
the dark and when the lights go out, I'm as wide-
awake as a car with its high beams on.

"Cal!" I cried, turning on my flashlight and
shining it across the room on Calvin. His face
looked calm, like bread baking in the machine.

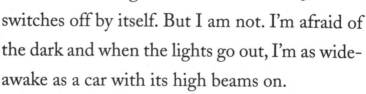

"Turn it off," said Calvin in a sleepy voice. "And go to sleep."

"But you just said—"

"I'm really tired," said Calvin. "And I don't want to talk about it."

Long silence.

"Why not?" I asked.

Calvin sniffed.

Silence.

Then Calvin sniffed again.

"Cal?" I said. "Are you crying?"

Calvin sniffed like crazy.

Calvin hardly ever cries. Not like me. I cry all the time. I like crying. But I think that Calvin does not.

"Do you want me to sleep with you?" I asked.

"Okay," squeaked Calvin.

So I hopped out of my bed and jumped into Calvin's.

It was very warm in Calvin's bed, not like mine, which is always very cold. And Calvin himself was like bread in the oven. But he smelled like soap.

"Don't worry, Cal," I said, putting my arm around his middle. "GungGung's gonna live for three hundred years."

"He's not," sobbed Calvin. "No one lives for that long."

"Well, maybe GungGung will," I said. "He's already halfway there."

"But the human brain shrinks with age," said Calvin.

"So?" I asked.

"So if GungGung lives to be three hundred," said Calvin, "his brain will be the size of a walnut."

Silence.

"Is that bad?" I asked.

"Bad?" cried Calvin, hugging his pillow. "It's horrible!" Then he really cried. *"Waaaaaah!"*

There's no fooling Calvin, that's for sure.

Poor Calvin.

And when Calvin cries like that, I cry too.

"Waaaaaaaaaaaaaaaaaaaaaaaah!"

Then we cried ourselves to sleep.

.●.●.

That night I had a dream that GungGung and I were on our way to Charlie Chow Fun's funeral.

Up the street we went, hand in hand. People came out of their shops and greeted us.

"What a brave boy," said the cookie maker.

"Courageous," said the mail carrier.

"He deserves a medal," said the sandwich lady.

I kept my head down.

I kept my hand in GungGung's hand.

We hurried along.

As we got closer to the cemetery, I began to see Charlie's face everywhere—in the trees, in the clouds, in the shop windows, on the parking meters.

"I'm not brave," I wanted to tell GungGung. "I'm not courageous. I'm not coming along nicely. I don't want to come along at all. I just want to go home."

But I couldn't.

Nothing came out of my mouth.

At the cemetery, everyone stepped aside to let us through. Hand in hand, we walked to the front where—there was—the casket.

And next to the casket was a big picture of— gasp!—my gunggung!

I wanted to ask GungGung what his picture was doing next to Charlie's coffin, but when I looked up, I wasn't holding GungGung's hand at all, I was holding Charlie Chow Fun's!

"I'm sorry about your gunggung," Charlie began.

That's when my heart exploded and I sat up with a start.

BEEEEP-BEEEEP-BEEEEP! The alarm was going off like my heart. It was time to get up for school.

CHAPTER SIX

Death Omens

dreaming that my gunggung had died was a sign from Above, I was sure of it.

"I need a sick day," I moaned, coming into the kitchen, where my dad was packing our lunches. Unfortunately, he's harder to fool than my mom, who had already left to drop off Anibelly at day care.

"Are you sick?" asked my dad.

"Urrrrrrr," I groaned.

My dad stopped. He looked at me.

"Sick days are for being sick," said my dad.

I groaned a little scarier.

But my dad didn't even put down his mustard knife. It was not a good sign.

"Maybe I need a personal day," I tried.

"A *personal* day?" asked my dad.

"Isn't that what you do, Dad?" asked Calvin, slurping down the last of his cereal. "When you don't have any excuses but you want to stay home from work anyway?"

My dad stopped.

A drop of mustard went *splat* on the counter.

My dad looked like he wanted to have a word with Calvin, but he had a few words for me instead.

"If you take a personal day from school," he said, "I assure you, you'll be getting lots of personal attention from me."

Gulp.

"C'mon," said my dad. "I'll *personally* take you to the bus stop today."

It's a good thing he did. I never would have made it out of the house on my own after a bad dream like that, that's for sure.

I never would have made it onto the school bus either.

My dad even stayed to watch my bus pull away like it was full of convicts going to prison.

Then I sat down next to Flea. *Phumph.* She's a girl. But all the other seats were already taken. It was my normal seat anyway, unfortunately.

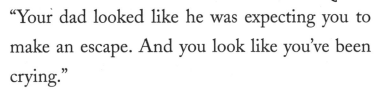

"Did you rob a bank or something?" Pinky asked, turning in his seat when the bus rounded the corner. "Your dad looked like he was expecting you to make an escape. And you look like you've been crying."

I shrank. Pinky's the biggest boy in my class and the leader of the gang on account of he started kindergarten late, and I'm the smallest boy and the leader of none. So normally, I'm not even on his radar.

"I had a bad dream," I said.

"A BAD DREAM?" shrieked Pinky, falling back into his seat and roaring his evil, wicked laugh. *"BWAHAHAHAHAHAHAHAHAHA!"*

The noise on the bus went round and round.

The wipers on the bus went *woop, woop, woop.*

But Pinky's voice still came in loud and clear.

"You're scared of a BAD DREAM???" Pinky hollered. "A WEE LITTLE SCAREDY DREEEEEAM???"

Oooh. It really shook my soda can.

"YOU'D HAVE A BAD DREAM TOO IF YOU WERE GOING TO A FUNERAL!" I burst.

Pinky stopped.

He stared at me.

His mouth opened, but nothing came out.

He looked so impressed that you'd think I was a fourteen-pound salmon.

"You're going to a funeral?" asked Scooter.

I nodded.

"A *real* funeral?" asked Eli.

I nodded again.

"One with a dead body?" asked Hobson.

"The works," I said.

Sam whistled. "Man," he said.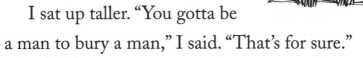
"You gotta be brave to go to
one of those."

I sat up taller. "You gotta be
a man to bury a man," I said. "That's for sure."

"Dude," said Scooter respectfully.

"Dude," said Jules solemnly.

"Dude." I swallowed.

"How'd you get invited?" asked Nhia. "Normally, kids aren't allowed at funerals."

"I invited myself," I said. My words floated
like shiny balloons above my head.

Mouths opened.

Eyes blinked.

So I sent up the shiniest balloon of all.

"My dad says I'm a hero," I said, puffing
out my chest.

The heads on the bus nodded up and down.

The eyes on the bus grew big and round.

Everyone was very impressed.

Everyone, that is, except Pinky. He was jealous.

"You're not a hero," he sneered. "You're a scaredy-cat. I bet you're making it up."

"I am not!" I cried.

"I bet you'll chicken out," said Pinky. "I bet you're not going to go at all."

"Am too!" I said.

"Are not!"

"Am too!"

"Are not!"

I stopped.

What was I saying? Not only was I getting closer and closer to that funeral by the minute, I was pushing myself right into the grave! Worse, now I really couldn't tell anyone how freaked out I was!

I sat back down. When you regret something that you've said, count to ten, my dad says, and keep your mouth shut. It's one of the rules of being a gentleman, I think, but I can't be sure. I don't remember. So I counted to ten and a half, just in case.

"Who died?" asked Flea, who'd been unusually quiet. Usually, she has a lot to say. And girls, as everyone knows, ask dumb questions that have nothing to do with what you're talking about.

"My gunggung's fr—" I began, but Jules interrupted.

"Are you going to the wake too?" asked Jules.

"What wake?"

"It's the night before the funeral," said Jules. "That's when you sit around and wait for the dead person to wake."

I gasped. GungGung didn't say anything about that.

"If the dead person wakes," Jules continued, "everyone goes to the pub to celebrate and that's the end of that. But if the corpse doesn't sit up and say, 'Hey, I'm hungry, let's get something to eat,' then you go to the pub anyway to celebrate without 'im—but some people might drag 'im along anyway."

My ears buzzed.

My eyes crossed.

The toast and milk in my stomach went up and down.

I clutched my PDK, which contains all sorts of useful items for surviving emergency situations, but nothing for waking a dead guy to go to the pub, that's for sure.

"Have you ever been to a funeral?" Flea asked.

I shook my head no.

"I didn't think so," said Flea. "I have. And I can tell you there's nothing to worry about."

I looked sideways at Flea. If there were anyone on the bus that I would have guessed had been to a funeral, it would have been Flea. She wears an eye patch over a blind eye and has one leg that is longer than the other, which she swings like a real peg leg. If there's anything good about Flea, it's this. She was born into piracy. And pirates, as everyone knows, plunder and kill, which means that they must go to funerals too.

"If you have any questions, just ask me," said Flea, thumping herself on the chest. "I'll give you the four-one-one." Her eye blinked. Maybe she was giving me a wink, but it's hard to tell when there's not another eye to compare it to.

"A lot of people are uncomfortable talking about deadly circumstances," Flea continued. "But I'm not. You know, been there, done that."

Just as I'd thought.

"Was . . . it . . . the funeral . . . creepy?" I asked.

"No," said Flea. "It was for my grandma. And it was really beautiful."

"Beautiful?" I said.

"There were flowers all over the place," said Flea. "My granny loved flowers."

That didn't sound too creepy.

"And the music was fantastic," said Flea. "They played my granny's favorite songs, the ones that she liked singing along to in the car."

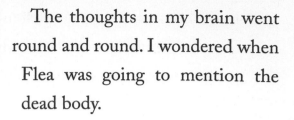

The thoughts in my brain went round and round. I wondered when Flea was going to mention the dead body.

"I was really sad at first," said Flea. "But the music made her come back to life again, and I could hear her singing at the top of her lungs while she drove me to the mall."

Dead people drive? That sure explained a lot of things. Like the time I went with my dad to the DMV and a bunch of dead-looking people were waiting in line for their licenses. Maybe Flea's granny was one of them and I didn't even know it!

"My granny was a very nice lady and everyone had special things to say about her," said Flea. "And their stories about her made her even more alive than the music did."

Yikes!

"Did your granny really die?" asked Ophelia. "Or is she leading tours in her house like Louisa May Alcott?"

"She's really dead," Flea said, suddenly

gloomy. "The saddest part was when they closed her coffin at the end and she didn't get out."

Then Flea got very, very quiet.

"She didn't even try," said Flea, wiping a tear from her eye.

The girls said they were sorry Flea lost her granny, which was a really weird thing to say when Flea's granny wasn't lost at all. She was buried at the cemetery under a stone with her name and telephone number on it.

Wasn't she?

"Did you get any signs that your granny was going to die?" I asked Flea.

"Signs?" asked Flea.

"You know, from Above." I rolled my eyes upward, like in prayer.

Flea's head tipped with the thought.

"You mean like an omen?" she asked.

"What's an omen?" I asked.

"It's a message," said Flea, "but not written with words."

"Oh," I said.

"You never want to get one of those," said Flea. "They're bad luck."

"Bad luck?"

"Real bad," said Flea. "Once they start, you'll begin to see signs all over the place. It's like the entire universe knows something and is shouting it to you."

"Like when a picture falls off the wall for no reason," said Sara Jane, "it means the person in the picture will die."

"Or if you see a clock that stops suddenly," said Eli, "it means your time is up."

"In India," said Esha, "seeing an owl during daylight means that someone in your family will die within the year."

"I've heard of people 'cheating' death," said Ophelia.

"What's that?" I asked.

"I think it's like cheating on a test," said Ophelia. "You've gotten a D for death, but you change it to an A for alive, when nobody's looking."

"How do you do that?" I asked.

"Well, when Death comes, you gotta look like someone younger," said Ophelia. "You can't look dead. You gotta sit up straight."

"Oh," I said, sitting as straight as a chopstick.

"My grandpa said that the surest sign of death is to dream of a birth or a wedding," said Nhia. "You can't cheat that."

"A dream?" My voice cracked like bone.

"I'd definitely die if I dreamt I got married," said Pinky.

"Me too," said Eli.

"What if you dream of a funeral?" I asked.

Silence.

The eyes on the bus went left and right.

The windows on the bus went *clackity-clack*.

This was how it was for the rest of the ride to school.

It was the worst sign of all.

CHAPTER SEVEN

"Alvin's Going to a Funeral."

this is what happens when I arrive at school.

My tongue is stuck like a pincushion with a thousand pins.

My mouth fills with sand.

My heart buzzes like a hummingbird's.

I make no eye contact.

"Alvin? Alvin Ho?"

It was Miss P. She's our second-grade teacher and she's very nice. But she has a habit of calling on

you when you least expect it, which is all the time.

"Can you tell us something about the Algonkians that was different from the Puritans?" asked Miss P.

Algonkians and Puritans?

Silence.

Weren't they the names of Little League teams that Calvin's team had played against? One wore red and the other wore green? I wasn't sure. I couldn't remember.

But I can tell you that Miss P's hair looks like cornsilk when she walks by the windows and she smells like fresh laundry every day, especially when she's standing next to your desk. This I can remember even with my eyes closed.

But my eyes were not closed. They were wide open to show that I was paying attention, which her letter to the Parents of Alvin Ho said that I needed to work on.

I'll show her.

I made Ping-Pong ball eyes.

They stared at her shoes (to avoid eye contact).

I kept my hands in plain sight.

"Alvin?" said Miss P, gently. She's very fair. She always gives me a chance to answer even though she knows my voice didn't make it to school with me.

Silence.

Then something long and boneless like an octopus tentacle waved above my head. It was Flea's arm. She's my desk buddy and she sits next to me in class.

"I know! I know!" said Flea eagerly.

"Yes, Sophie," said Miss P, using Flea's real name.

"The Algonkians made their clothes from the skins of deer and moose and beaver and other wild animals," said Flea, breathlessly. "And from the feathers of birds too."

"That's right," said Miss P, smiling and nodding at Flea. "And what did the Puritans make their clothes from?"

"Cloth," said Flea. "They were vegetarian."

Miss P smiled. "The Puritans fished, hunted and trapped for food," she said.

"Oh," said Flea, disappointed.

"What else was different between the Algonkians and Puritans?" Miss P asked, looking around. "This question will be on your history test, and you'll need to remember one difference between them."

Esha waved.

"When an Algonkian died, they grieved by painting their faces and wailing in mourning ceremonies," she said. "Puritan funerals were quick and quiet, without the fancy stuff."

"Excellent," said Miss P.

Then Sara Jane's hand shot up.

"Alvin's going to a funeral," announced Sara

Jane, sounding like she was giving helpful information.

"Oh?" said Miss P, turning and looking at me with more concern than before. "Who died, Alvin?"

"His gunggung," said Scooter, answering for me.

"Alvin told us on the bus," said Nhia.

"Yup," said Sam, nodding sadly.

Miss P gasped.

I froze.

"I'm so sorry, Alvin," said Miss P. "I had no idea."

I had no idea either. I wanted to tell Miss P that they had gotten it all wrong. It wasn't my gunggung who had died, but his friend. But I couldn't. My lips were stapled shut.

"I didn't get a chance to meet your grandpa," said Miss P, "but I know that he was one of our grandparent volunteers in the library."

I wrapped my feet around the legs of my desk.

I kept my hands in plain sight.

"Mr. Kemp will be very sad to get your news," Miss P continued. "I'll let him know as soon as I can."

"MY GUNGGUNG IS OKAY!" I wanted to scream. "HE DIDN'T DIE! HE'S STILL ALIVE!!!!!" But nothing came out of my mouth.

My vocal cords grew hair.

And the hair tangled into a hairball.

I gagged silently.

Everything in the room faded to gray.

"Was Alvin's grandpa Algonkian or Puritan?" Ophelia asked.

"Neither," said Miss P. "I think that he was Chinese, and the Chinese have their own funeral traditions."

Silence.

"I'm so sorry, Alvin," Miss P said again. "I'll write your parents a note and send it home with you tonight."

I was so sorry too. My dad always says, "The sooner you tell someone about a mistake, the less trouble there'll be for you later."

So right there and then I could smell trouble coming at me like a fox going after a chicken egg.

I blinked.

Was this another death omen? After all, how can so many people mistakenly think that my gunggung has died unless—gasp!—he's actually about to die?

I swallowed. I breathed in. I breathed out. I did my best not to cry. But before I knew it I was crying full blast like a fire hydrant in an emergency! *"Waaaaaaaaaaaaaaaaaaaaaaaaaaaaaaaaah!"*

CHAPTER EIGHT

Paper Houses

crying in school has its advantages:

You get to go to the nurse's office for a time-out.

You get as many bathroom passes as you want.

The lunch ladies give you free chocolate milk.

Everyone is super-duper nice to you.

Best of all, the rest of the day goes by in a blur. Usually.

But this was not usual. There was a terrible

misunderstanding. So nothing blurred . . . and when nothing blurs, you can see clearly the many *disadvantages* to crying in school:

The principal stops you at recess and says, "I'm very sorry, Alvin."

You had no idea that the principal even knew your name.

The principal says, "Your grandpa was a very kind and generous man. We're all going to miss him very much."

The principal tries to talk to you some more. You freak out.

You run away as fast as you can.

You see your gunggung's face everywhere as you zip down the hall—on the coat hooks, in the windows, on the stairs and even on a gum wrapper on the floor!

And just when you think you've outrun her, you turn and see that the principal is still following you. Yikes!

Quick, I slipped into the library. There are places to hide in the library. Plus, it's the only place where it's perfectly okay to not talk at all, which makes it the only safe place for me in the whole, entire school. In fact, Mr. Kemp, our librarian, says I'm the library's best bookworm on account of I'm as silent as a worm.

I clutched my PDK and slid behind a low shelf and rolled myself into the smallest ball that I could, in the farthest corner away from everything.

I squeezed my eyes shut.

I felt the soft carpet under me.

I wiggled my anterior.

Then I wiggled my posterior.

Ahem. The most embarrassing thing about being a worm is that it's hard to tell the difference between my head and my butt. But everything else rocks.

I'm very muscular.

And slimy.

I can tell when it's going to rain.

I can feel vibrations in the air.

"We should do something to honor him," said a vibration. It was Mr. Kemp.

"He started volunteering here when his

daughter was a student," said another vibration. Gasp! It was Miss Madhaven, the principal.

"It would be nice if the children could celebrate his life," said Mr. Kemp. "We could have a Chinese ceremony for him."

"I thought of that too," said Miss Madhaven. "I tried to speak to Alvin about it, but he ran away before I could say anything."

"The little fellow must be in shock," said Mr. Kemp.

"Terrible shock," said Miss Madhaven. "I understand that his classmates are sad for him too."

"I'm planning a special activity for his class today," said Mr. Kemp.

"That's a good idea," said Miss Madhaven. "And we'll have a little memorial service with them tomorrow."

I opened my eyes in time to see Miss Madhaven march out and Miss P march in with the whole class behind her. Everyone was clutching their books to return, everyone, that is, except me. I can never remember when library day is, so all of my books were still at home. But I clutched my PDK and popped out of my hiding place and right into my spot at the end of the line.

"Welcome to library hour," said Mr. Kemp.

My anterior went up.

"I have good news and bad news," Mr. Kemp continued. "The bad news is that Alvin lost his grandfather, as you all know."

That was a weird thing to say. I thought that he thought that my gunggung was dead, not lost.

Heads turned.

"I'm very sorry, Alvin," said Mr. Kemp, his voice cracking like dried leftover rice. "I miss him terribly, and I know you miss him even more."

I pulled in my anterior and my posterior.

I kept my PDK in plain sight.

"IT'S ALL A MISTAKE!" I wanted to shout, but I couldn't. Worms have no vocal cords. But worms have five hearts, which, when they pump like crazy, hurt like crazy, which made me want to set the record straight once and for all and lead an honest life.

"Your classmates will miss him too," Mr. Kemp continued. "Your grandpa has been reading to them during story hour since kindergarten."

It was true. My gunggung doesn't come every week, but he takes turns with the other grandparents.

"This class will have a special memorial service for Alvin's gunggung tomorrow," said Mr. Kemp.

A memorial service? What's that? A funeral for someone who isn't dead yet?

"So today we will read about Chinese funeral traditions and then do a craft project for tomorrow's ceremony," said Mr. Kemp.

"MY GUNGGUNG ISN'T DEAD!" I wanted to scream, but my mouth had filled with clay.

Worse, Mr. Kemp began reading creepy stuff about Chinese funerals:

" 'The Chinese believe that funerals are filled with bad omens and bad spirits trying to trade places with the new dead person in the after-life.' "

Yikes!

" 'When the family leaves for the funeral, every light in the house must be turned on to help the deceased find his or her way out. . . .

" 'Once they leave the house for the funeral, the Chinese do not look back, which they believe will point death into the house again. And no one returns home for any reason until the service is over, for fear of leading the deceased back to be trapped.' "

No wonder Concord has so many dead authors stuck in their homes leading tours!

" 'During the wake, friends of the deceased gamble near the coffin while they're guarding the corpse; the gambling helps the guards stay awake all night—' "

"Mr. Kemp," Flea interrupted.

Mr. Kemp stopped. He looked up from his book.

"Alvin hasn't breathed since you started reading," said Flea. "I think he's all freaked out."

Everyone turned.

Maybe I was freaked out, and maybe I wasn't. Who could tell? I was wearing my emergency scary mask to scare away all the scary thoughts.

"Alvin?" said Mr. Kemp. "Are you okay, Alvin?"

Silence.

Fortunately, Mr. Kemp is a very good librarian. He has a laser gun for checking out books, and an ink pad for fingerprinting criminals. He can read books facing away from him as though they were not. And he knows when to stop reading and take out his hot-glue gun.

Making a craft, as everyone knows, can calm you down. And it can help you remember a story better.

So I put away my mask.

I cut.

I pasted.

I colored.

We were making paper houses and filling them with paper furniture and paper food and paper money. Paper cars went into the paper garages. Paper logs into the paper fireplaces.

"The Chinese believe that they can make the afterlife comfortable for their loved ones by making paper symbols of things that they'll need," said Mr. Kemp. "So they make paper houses and fill them with useful things. Then they burn these at the funeral, and the smoke is believed to carry everything to heaven."

My scissors stopped in midair.

"Alvin's gunggung's gonna have SO MANY houses in heaven!" cried Flea, eyeballing everyone's craft project with her one good eye.

"And baseballs too!" said Nhia, putting a paper baseball and glove in his paper house. "He loved baseball."

"Yeah," said Sam, cutting a pile of little rectangles. "I'm giving him season tickets to the Red Sox."

My paste dried up.

My crayons rolled away.

Paper houses for the afterlife? It was the creepiest craft ever!

Worse, it was another omen, I was sure of it. If my gunggung wasn't about to die, why would we be making him paper houses?

I turned ghostly cold.

Something dribbled out of my nose.

I had a bad sinking feeling that I was headed for so much trouble, I needed to save my paper house for myself!

CHAPTER NINE

Paying Respects to the Widow

i was getting closer and closer to that creepy funeral, but first there was going to be a memorial service for my gunggung, who wasn't dead yet, and if my mom and dad ever found out about it, there'd be another funeral—mine!

So I shut my eyes.

And hurried home.

When the bus dropped me off, I flew up my driveway and burst into my house.

"HIIIIMOMMIMHOMMME!!!" I

yelled. "ISITOKAYIFIGOTOPOHPOHAND-
GUNGGUNG'SHOUSE?"

It was one of those days when my mom was
working from home, which meant that my
gunggung was hanging out at his own house. My
mom and Anibelly and Lucy were
doing Yoga Without Pain
in front of the TV.

Oooh, I love Yoga
Without Pain. But I
had no time for it.

"That would be fine, darling," said my mom
in upward dog. "How was school today?"

I stopped dead in my tracks.

I love it when she calls me that. Darling. I
love it more than my own name. I felt like giving
her one hundred and thirty-two kisses. But I
didn't. It would have messed up my plans to go
to my grandparents' house.

"School?" I said. "What school?"

Silence.

Oops.

My mom moved from upward dog into watchdog, which is a special bonus feature not on the video.

"Is everything okay at school?"

I didn't breathe in.

I didn't breathe out.

I couldn't lie. It isn't my thing. But I couldn't tell her the truth either.

So Anibelly did. She always tells it like it is.

"You don't look okay to me," said Anibelly. She twisted sideways like a rubber band. "You look like you've seen a scary movie or something."

Then my mom looked at me in that way that sees down to the very bottom of me. She looked and looked. Then she wrapped her yoga arms around me and gave me a hug.

"Scary movie, indeed," said my mom. "I guess some days school can be the scariest movie of all."

I melted. I love it whenever she puts her arms around me. I love it more than candy.

My mom smiled. "Well, I'm sure your grand-parents will be very happy to see you," she said.

"Yup," I said. "And I'll be very happy to see them!"

I turned and dashed up the stairs.

"Remember your manners," my mom yelled after me. "Call ahead to let them know you're coming."

"Okay, Mom!" I yelled back.

But I was not okay. I hopped into my super-hero Firecracker Man outfit, the one that Gung-Gung himself had sewn for me. It was good for saving the world, and now it was coming in handy to save GungGung! And maybe . . . GungGung might even let me wear it to Charlie's funeral so that I could save myself from all the bad spirits.

"Bakbakbakbakbakbakbakbakbakbakbakbakbakbak!" I screamed, tearing around my room like a string of firecrackers.

Then I stopped dead in my tracks.

Normally when I'm in a panic, I ask Calvin what to do.

But Calvin wasn't home. He had stayed behind

at school for the philistine society, whatever that is. All I know is that it had something to do with soaking some envelopes in water to get the stamps off.

I ran to the window.

I looked down the driveway.

There was no Calvin anywhere.

So I thought and thought and thought, until my brain was nearly dead.

Then I made an emergency plan for helping GungGung:

How to Help Gung Gung Live to ~~122~~ 300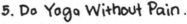

1. Make him exercise like crazy.
2. Walk.
3. Play catch.
4. Hang from the monkey bars.
5. Do Yoga Without Pain.
6. Feed him vegetables.
7. Broccoli.
8. Carrots.
9. Brussel sprouts.
10. Spinach.
11. Extra Spinach.

It was super-duper!

Then I added:

12. Don't let him cross the street.

Just in case.

It sure was a LOT of work! But after a while I tucked the emergency plan and emergency supplies into my PDK and hurried downstairs. There was no time to waste. GungGung's life was passing by the minute!

In the kitchen, my mom was talking on her cell phone and typing on her laptop and I could hear Anibelly's singing coming from the bathroom. "Lalalalalalalalalalala," she sang.

They were finished with Yoga Without Pain, so I popped out the DVD and slipped it into my PDK. Normally, I don't take my PDK to GungGung and PohPoh's house. But this was not normal. This was a matter of life and death!

"HEYMOMDOYOUMINDIFITAKE-SOMEVEGGIESTOGUNGGUNG?

HESURECOULDUSESOMEVEGGIES!" I
said.

"TAKE THEM," said my mom. I had to read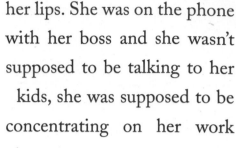
her lips. She was on the phone
with her boss and she wasn't
supposed to be talking to her
kids, she was supposed to be
concentrating on her work
or else!

I opened the refrigerator and pulled out the
vegetable drawer and dumped it into
my PDK—tomatoes, onions, carrots.
But the lettuce wouldn't fit.

"LalaLaLaLALALALALA."
Anibelly's singing suddenly grew
louder. She was coming out of the
bathroom.

If she saw me, I would get stuck taking her
along. I had to get away fast!

But oh no! My PDK was too heavy to carry!

Quick, I dropped everything, including the
lettuce head, into Anibelly's baby pram, the one
she uses to push her dolls around in, and slipped

out the kitchen door faster than a chipmunk with a nut.

I don't know if Anibelly saw me or not.

I didn't look back. I didn't dare.

I just kept going, full speed ahead, smokin' the tires on that baby carriage.

.•.•.

If I could travel to anyplace in the world, it would be to my gunggung and pohpoh's house.

It's not too far away. (But I can still hear a foreign language.)

I don't have to go through airport security. (But I do have to take off my shoes.)

I don't have to watch the scary emergency mask thing. (But I can watch one hundred and fifteen channels on command.)

I don't have to eat a dry little sandwich from a dry little box. (I get first-class service.)

Their toilet doesn't do that sucking thing that

you know is meant to vacuum you into outer space without anyone knowing so that the plane can lighten its load.

Best of all, PohPoh and GungGung's living room is Red Sox heaven. One wall is covered with Red Sox pennants, framed newspaper clippings of famous Red Sox games, autographed photos and an autographed Red Sox jersey. Another wall is painted like the Green Monster, complete with a scoreboard: NYY 0, Boston 6. The sofas and chairs are covered with Red Sox blankets and Fenway Green slipcovers and Red Sox pillows. Red Sox coasters and paperweights are on the tables. On the floor is a Red Sox rug that GungGung made from a kit. On the ceiling is a painting of Fenway Park that GungGung did all by himself, not from a kit. And when you're lying on the sofa looking up, it looks like you're right there in the stands!

All this I could see through the window on their front porch, where I was pounding on their door and ringing their bell like crazy.

"HEY, GUNGGUNG AND POHPOH, IT'S ME, ALVIN!" I screamed at the top of my lungs. "LEMME IN!"

It's normal for me to scream like this on account of it's polite to let people know you're coming. My mom would be proud that I remembered.

But it wasn't normal for me to not burst right in. One of them is always home, and their door is never locked.

"LEMME IN!" I tried again.

Silence.

I rattled their door.

It was locked.

And it was very, very quiet.

"PohPoh?" I whispered. "GungGung?"

I peeked in their window.

Nothing moved.

No one answered.

It was very strange. I'd never seen PohPoh and GungGung's house like this.

My chest tightened.

My liver flipped.

I blinked, hard. A tear fell on the front step as I sat down to think. The wooden step groaned. *Urrrrrrrrrrgh.*

Was this another omen? Flea's voice swirled in my ears. "It's like the entire universe knows something and is shouting it to you."

Raindrops began to stain the step where the paint had worn away. It had been raining off and on all day. And it was cold. I shivered in my Firecracker Man outfit, which is good for all seasons, but not particularly good for rain or swimming. And Anibelly's baby stroller looked slightly puzzled on the lawn with its vegetable passengers. I was puzzled too.

Where were PohPoh and GungGung?

Did one of them get sick?

If one of them was sick, why were they *both* gone?

Were they both sick?

Were they at the hospital?

Did an ambulance come for them?

Did the ambulance get here in time?

Was I too late with my emergency diet and exercise plan?

My heart jackhammered.

Raindrops ran down my face like tears.

Tears ran down my face like raindrops.

"*Waaaaaaaaaaaaaaaaaaaah!*" I wailed. "*Waaaaaaaaaaaaaaaah!*"

I hugged my knees and cried my eyes out.

Then suddenly the rain called out to me. "Alvin," it said in a soft, old voice.

I covered my ears. I didn't want to hear the universe telling me anything anymore. It was too creepy!

But I looked up.

It was GungGung! He was hurrying through the rain toward me, and PohPoh was with him.

"*Aiyaaah,* you look like a wet rat!" said Poh-Poh. Then she said some fast Chinese words to GungGung that sounded like he'd better pick up the wet rat quick and take it inside, or else!

"Where were you?" I cried as soon as we came into their warm kitchen.

"We went to pay our respects to Charlie's widow," said GungGung.

"What's the widow?" I asked.

"You poor thing," said Poh-Poh. "Change now, talk later."

Off went my shoes.

Off went my socks.

Off went my cold, wet Firecracker Man outfit.

On went a warm towel.

On went the teakettle.

On went a completely different outfit.

It was a jogging suit.

It's what PohPoh wears when she goes to the Y. I've seen her in it. It makes her look very sporty.

But it only made me look like PohPoh.

"Do I have to wear this?" I whined.

"Only until your outfit is dried," said Gung-Gung, throwing Firecracker Man into the dryer.

PohPoh was looking at me all funny and beaming. "You've grown, Alvin," she said. "You're almost my size now."

I looked in the mirror.

I'd never seen how clothes can change a person, but I saw it now. There we were—me and PohPoh—like a pair of exercise ladies at the Y, side by side.

"The jogging suit doesn't look bad on you," said GungGung. "Looks like you're ready for armchair aerobics."

The suit didn't look bad on me, but it didn't look good either. It was *pink,* with green palm trees all over it. And when I pulled the hood over my head, I really looked like an old granny. Yikes! I'd die if anyone saw me in it. But Gung-Gung was right. I looked ready for a workout, which made me suddenly remember . . .

"Let's go hit your treadmill, GungGung!" I said.

"Wearing the suit makes you want to exercise?" asked GungGung, looking at me. He knew that I knew that he knew that I was mostly allergic to exercise, just like he was. It makes us short of breath, turns our skin pink and gives us the sweats. Worse, it makes us tired.

I nodded.

"That's some suit," said GungGung.

"Wearing the right outfit is half the battle," said PohPoh, pouring tea and setting out her black sesame pudding on the kitchen table. "Snack first, exercise later."

TGFPP. Thank God for PohPoh. She always knows when I'm hungry even before I know I'm hungry. And I was starved!

"Charlie's widow was very sad," said Gung-Gung, digging into the sweet pudding.

"Charlie's black widow spider?" I asked.

"The wife of a man who died is called a widow," said GungGung. "And it's customary to pay your respects."

"How do you do that?" I asked, blowing on my favorite hot oolong tea.

"You go to her home and sit with her for a while," said GungGung.

"Is that all?"

"You could bring her food," said PohPoh. "People who are in mourning are often too sad to cook for themselves. Food is always appreciated."

"We brought her lasagna," said GungGung. "In China, we might have brought her a Chinese dish."

"Then what?" I asked.

"Then you just sit," said GungGung. "Depends on the widow's mood. She might cry. You might cry. Or you might have a memory to share with her. Mostly you just need to be sympathetic."

"Oh," I said. It didn't sound too creepy. But I had a feeling it was creepier than they were letting on.

So I asked, "Was the dead body there?"

GungGung's and PohPoh's teacups stopped in midair.

They looked at each other.

Neither of them said a word. PohPoh didn't even say any fast Chinese words that sounded like anything.

So that's how I knew that the dead body *was* there.

"Well, in China, the body is dressed in its finest and laid out in the home for visitors until the funer—" GungGung began.

But PohPoh cut him off with some super-duper fast Chinese words that sounded like GungGung had better not frighten me, or else! But I was already freaked out.

"PohPoh's old-fashioned Chinese," said GungGung. "She doesn't want me to talk about death. She thinks that it'll invite bad luck."

So GungGung didn't say any more.

Then PohPoh said some regular fast Chinese words that sounded like she was going to the grocery store so that she could make me a special

dinner and that GungGung had better do something fun with me like exercising.

So after we watched PohPoh's car pull out of
the driveway, GungGung said we could go to the
"dungeon" to walk on the treadmill or play Ping-
Pong.

"Yippeee!" I cried.

But on the way to the dungeon was a sofa.

The big Red Sox sofa.

GungGung's favorite.

For an afternoon nap.

"All that talk about exercise has tired me out,"
said GungGung, pulling on a Red
Sox cap. Then he put his feet up
and lowered his head onto a Red
Sox pillow, and pulled a Red Sox
blanket over himself.

"GungGung!" I cried. "You're supposed to
be hitting the treadmill, not the sofa!"

"But it's raining out," he said sleepily. "Such a
perfect, soporific afternoon. Why don't you take
the other sofa?"

"You can't nap now!" I cried.

"Nap first," said GungGung, closing his eyes. "Exercise later."

ZZZZZZzzzzzzzzz.

"But there's something I wanted to ask you," I wailed. "Will there be ghosts and creepy Chinese stuff at Charlie's funeral???"

ZZZZZZzzzzzzzzzz.

The problem with GungGung is that when he falls asleep, it's as quick as turning the page.

"Tell me now!" I cried. "Nap later!"

ZZZZZZZzzzzzzzzz.

It was too late. I slumped into the other sofa and pulled the hood over my head.

GungGung loves to nap. He normally naps at our house when he's supposed to be watching us. The good thing about his naps is that they're short. The bad thing is that there's nothing you can do to wake him. He's as dead as an old car battery.

Ding-dong!

I jumped. It was their front-door bell.

I ran to see who it was. I peered through the

lace curtain and spied some familiar figures standing on the front porch.

So I cracked open the door just a little.

"Hello, ma'am," said a voice I knew.

I gasped. It was Pinky! And behind him was the gang!

"We heard the bad news," Pinky continued politely, his eyes wandering along the floor. He didn't look normal. Normally, he's not polite and his eyes watch you like a king cobra watching a mongoose. "Our librarian sent us to invite you to a special memorial service."

Silence.

"And our parents said it would be good

manners for us to pay our last respects to you while we're at it," said Eli.

"We know Alvin from school," said Sam. "And we know GungGung from the library."

"He was a gunggung to everyone," added Nhia.

I froze.

I could hardly believe my ears.

Or my eyes.

There was the gang with their heads hanging down, looking as sad as a bunch of broken toys.

And there I was, standing on the other side of the door, in *granny clothes*.

Oops.

If I let them in, there was going to be trouble.

If I turned them away, word would get out that my pohpoh was unfriendly, which she is not. She's a very nice lady.

"Did you bring food?" I asked in my best granny voice.

Silence.

Then there were whispers.

Then silence again.

"No, ma'am." Sam spoke up this time, his voice shaking a little. "None of us has ever done this b-b-before and we didn't know we were s-s-supposed to bring anything."

"But we have some pieces of c-c-candy between us," said Eli, who always has candy in his pockets.

"Fine," I said, putting a granny cackle into my voice. "I'll take the candy."

I opened the door wider.

The gang stepped in. Their mouths opened and their eyes fell out.

"Wow," said Hobson.

"It's better than the gift shop," said Nhia.

"It's not Fenway Park," whispered Scooter. "It's Fenway Paradise."

"When I die," whispered Sam, "this is where I want to go."

"Dude," said Eli, nodding. "Me too."

Then they stopped dead in their tracks.

They didn't see him at first on account of it's hard to notice someone tucked in among all the razzle-dazzle. But they saw him now.

Straight in front of them on the sofa was GungGung, laid out in his finest Red Sox gear. He not only looked dead, he looked much more than that.

"You can leave your candies on the table there," I croaked from behind the door. "It's very kind of you boys to come."

"Is th-th-that his actual real d-d-dead body?" asked Nhia.

I kept my head down. I made no eye contact.

"My m-m-mom says we should s-s-sit quietly," stuttered Pinky, pressing himself against the wall as far away from GungGung as possible. "And that we sh-sh-shouldn't stay long."

"No, n-n-not long at all," said Scooter.

"And if you're not in the m-m-mood to talk to us, we won't s-s-say anything at all," said Eli.

"We're supposed to be simply p-p-pathetic," said Sam.

Silence.

"Sure is n-n-nice he died with his Red Sox c-c-cap on," said Hobson.

Silence.

I kept my head down.

The gang kept their heads down.

"I've never s-s-seen a real live dead b-b-body before," said Nhia.

"I've never b-b-been in the s-s-same room with one," said Sam.

I sniffed.

The gang sniffed.

I made a little whimper.

The gang made a little whimper.

"Is that all the candy you've got?" I squeaked in my best granny voice.

Several more pieces landed on the table.

It was perfect!

Then I began to cry, softly at first, then louder and louder until I was wailing like a siren going to an emergency.

The gang wailed too.

They were very simply pathetic.

Suddenly my gunggung sat up. His eyes popped out like hard-boiled eggs. This is how he normally wakes from a nap at my house, like a zombie bolting from the grave, on account of he knows he shouldn't be sleeping on the job. And his nap was over, just like that.

"*AAAAAAAAAAAAAAAAAAAAAAAAAAA AAAAAAAAAAAAAAAAAAAAAAAAAAAAAA AAAAAAAAAAAAAAAAAAAAAAAAAAACK!*" screamed the gang.

I don't think that I need to tell you what happened after that.

CHAPTER TEN

How to Write a Condolence Letter

when you've seen a corpse rise from the dead the way the gang's seen it, my dad would call it a game-changer. It's a move that turns everything around. If you were losing, you'd start winning. If you were in jail, you'd get out of jail free.

If you had thought that my gunggung was dead, you'd now know that he was alive, and you'd tell the teacher, who'd tell the librarian, who'd tell the principal, who'd cancel the memorial service, right?

Wrong.

The game changed, all right.

It made GungGung a great deal deader.

"D-d-don't hurt me," stuttered Pinky when I got on the bus the next morning. "I like d-d-dead people."

"I'm always nice to dead people!" said Hobson when I walked past.

"Met like never I a person didn't dead I," said Scooter, which made no sense at all.

"I'll do a-a-anything you ask," said Pinky. "A-a-anything."

Heads nodded.

Wow. It was a dream come true!

I didn't know what to say.

What do you say when suddenly you're practically the leader of the gang?

Well, there's a lot of things you can say.

"Carry my backpack."

"Velcro my shoes."

"Do my homework."

"Gimme candy."

"Eat my PDK."

So I did. I said all those things.

But the one thing I couldn't say, which I wanted to say more than anything else, was the truth.

"MY GUNGGUNG'S NOT DEAD!" I wanted to shout. I needed to explain everything while I still could. As soon as I got to school, my voice would be gone, and so would my chance to stop the memorial service.

But I couldn't.

It would have ruined everything. My gung-gung would be a regular dude again, and I'd be regular too. And regular dudes, as everyone knows, don't get the same respect as zombie-dudes. Worse, I'd be known for wearing you-know-what.

So I didn't.

I didn't make anything right. And when you do that, you're really in for it.

•••••

"Alvin?" said a voice. "Alvin Ho?"

It was Miss P. She's very nice and smells like fresh laundry every day. But she has a habit of calling on you when you're just about to make history as the first boy to blast out of school and straight into outer space.

"You look like you would have a wonderful example of a homophone to share with us," said Miss P.

She smiled like the morning sun.

I fell out of my space shuttle like a bird out of its nest, and landed—*thud!*—right on my butt.

I'm a wonderful example of what?

"Ho-mo-phone," whispered Flea, who was sitting next to me, and who was always trying to be helpful.

"Homophones are words that sound alike," said Miss P. "But they could be spelled differently or spelled the same, and have different meanings."

I knew that. Sort of.

Miss P wrote two words on the board:

Flea flee

Sam's hand went up. "The first one is Flea's name," he said. "And the second means you run away."

"Good, Sam," said Miss P.

Then the class came up with more homophones, which Miss P wrote on the board:

Miss P was very pleased. "Homophones are very useful in making puns and understanding jokes," she said. "You can make a collection of them. They're little gems in our language."

Flea's arm shot up. "I have another one," she said.

Miss P smiled and readied her chalk on the board.

"Morning, as in when we wake up," said Flea. "And mourning, as in . . ."

Flea stopped. I could feel her head turning toward me. Then I felt her one good eye on me.

Then all heads turned.

All eyes were on me.

"Mourning is the deep sadness we feel when someone dies," said Miss P, writing the two words on the board. "You can say that our class is in mourning for Alvin's grandpa."

Silence.

Flea made a sad eye. Her lips turned downward. Although she's a pirate, she had spent more time working on her Chinese calligraphy with my gunggung in our kitchen than anyone else.

"Do people mourn for the undead?" asked Scooter.

"The undead?" asked Miss P.

"You know, like the dead authors who are still in their homes," said Scooter.

"We went over to Alvin's gunggung's place to pay our respects yesterday," said Eli.

"Turns out he didn't go to regular heaven," said Scooter. "He got himself into Red Sox heaven."

"He died with his Red Sox cap on," said Hobson. "Then he rose from the dead."

"Rose from the dead?" Miss P wrinkled her forehead.

"Just like Ralph Waldo Emerson," said Pinky with awe in his voice.

"But that's an actor," said Miss P.

Silence.

"Are you all feeling okay?" Miss P asked.

Silence.

If this were a normal town, this kind of news

would definitely be a game-changer. Miss P would get on the phone and tell the principal, who would tell the librarian to cancel the memorial service. And that would be the end of that. But because this isn't a normal town, and many undead people hang around, charging admission and giving tours of their homes, the news only changed one thing. Our lesson.

"I'm so sorry," said Miss P. "I should have realized how hard this was on all of you. Instead of diving right into our lesson, we should have done something more appropriate. . . .

"This is a wonderful chance for us to use our letter-writing skills to write condolences to Alvin's family," continued Miss P. "It would be a kind and thoughtful gesture to let the family know that you're thinking of them and will miss their loved one too."

"Will Alvin write a letter to himself?" asked Flea.

"Alvin can write to his grandma," said Miss P. "I'm sure that she'll be very touched."

Then Miss P wrote this on the board:

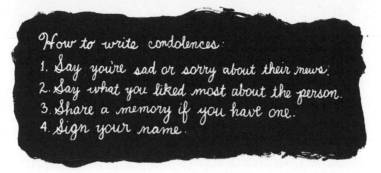

How to write condolences:
1. Say you're sad or sorry about their news.
2. Say what you liked most about the person.
3. Share a memory if you have one.
4. Sign your name.

Normally, I'm pretty allergic to letter writing. I never know what to say. But now I was *severely* allergic! What do I say to PohPoh when Gung-Gung is supposed to be dead, but isn't?

~~Dear PohPoh,~~
~~I'm sorry that you're going to kill me.~~

~~Dear PohPoh,~~
~~I'm sad that I'm going to die when you read this~~

~~Dear PohPoh,~~
~~It was really nice being your grandson~~

I could hardly get started. But before I knew it, there was a stack of letters on Miss P's desk, just like that. Then she took a white ribbon from the

 art cabinet and tied it neatly around the letters, which made them look like a gift.

"We'll present these to your family at the end of the service," said Miss P.

We will?

"Alvin, you did remember to give your parents my letter inviting them to join us this afternoon, didn't you?" asked Miss P.

I made no eye contact.

I kept my hands in plain sight.

Letter? What letter?

CHAPTER ELEVEN

Like She'd Seen a Ghost

this is how you know you've dug your own grave.

Mr. Kemp was all dressed up. In a suit. His hair was combed.

The library was neat and tidy.

Cookies sat on trays on tablecloth-covered tables. Fresh flowers and paper houses sat next to the cookies.

Grandparent volunteers smiled at us as we marched into the library after Miss P and sat down at our usual places on the carpet in front of the fake fireplace for story hour.

Then Calvin came in.

"I invited your brother to join us today," said Mr. Kemp. "I thought he'd want to be here."

It sure didn't look like he wanted to be here to me.

Calvin stood against the back wall. He looked like he'd been crying. His eyes were red and puffy. He kept wiping his nose on his sleeve. He was a mess!

Then I remembered something. His fourth-grade class had gone on a field trip yesterday. And I'd forgotten to mention to him that there was a mix-up at school about GungGung being dead.

Oops.

"Good morning," said Mr. Kemp.

Everyone quieted.

"Thank you for coming today to celebrate the life of a man who has been an important part of our school for more than thirty years," said Mr. Kemp.

My insides tightened.

My head spun.

My throat closed.

But surprise, surprise—Mr. Kemp made a really nice speech. It wasn't creepy at all. In fact, I learned a few things about my gunggung that I didn't know before:

He'd taught Chinese calligraphy during 生命 library hours.

A few times he demonstrated tai chi sword.

Once, he brought in treasures from his Red Sox collection for show-and-tell. But only once.

How I missed all that, I had no idea— I always go to library hour.

Then a couple of the grandparent volunteers made speeches.

"He was the one who badgered me to start coming here to read to the kids," said a lady. "It changed my life."

"He sure loved the Red Sox," said a man. "And I sure loved his Red Sox collection. I hope he didn't take it all with him."

Everyone laughed.

It wasn't what I had expected at all. There was nothing creepy about a memorial service. There wasn't even a dead body.

Best of all, Miss P had postponed our history test for another day.

But Calvin mostly cried. He couldn't stop. Poor Calvin.

Then the principal stood up.

"I know this class was very special to Alvin's gunggung," Miss Madhaven began.

Just then the library door opened.

In walked GungGung!

"Wow, the library looks nice today," he said.

There were gasps.

"Who died?" he asked, looking at all the paper houses.

I'm not sure who was the first to scream, but I think it might have been the principal, like she'd seen a ghost or something.

Cookies flew.

Paper houses collapsed.

Punch spilled.

There was a stampede for the exit.

The only ones who ran toward GungGung were me and Calvin.

I'm always glad to see my gunggung, and Calvin was extra-super-duper happy to see him.

CHAPTER TWELVE

A Bucket List

there was quite a lot of explaining to do when I got home. GungGung wanted to hear how a memorial service for him had come about. Calvin and Anibelly listened for a while, then they got bored and went upstairs. I was glad they did, on account of there were some scary parts that wouldn't have been suitable for Anibelly to hear. Then I told it all to GungGung the best I could and didn't leave out anything, not even my very bad dream or the creepy stuff I'd learned about Chinese funerals, especially not that.

GungGung nodded. He listened quietly. We were in the kitchen enjoying a cup of tea (his) and a glass of milk (mine). And when I was done, he smiled.

"Well, that explains a lot of things," he said. Then he called the principal and explained it all to her.

"Is she mad?" I asked.

"No," said GungGung. "She understood completely."

"Are you mad?" I asked.

"Mad?" asked GungGung. "Why should I be mad?"

"These were all unlucky signs that you're going to . . . to . . . to . . ."

"Die?" asked GungGung.

I nodded.

"I think that they're all *lucky* signs," said GungGung. "They showed that people really care about me."

"But aren't you afraid of dying?" I asked. "Or . . . going to Charlie's funeral?"

GungGung looked at me.

He leaned closer.

"I'm a little bit afraid of going to Charlie's funeral," GungGung whispered.

"You are?"

GungGung nodded. "When you've known someone for more than eighty years, saying goodbye is a really big deal," he said. "It's like cutting off a part of yourself. And I'm afraid of how much it's going to hurt."

"Oh," I said. I hadn't thought of that.

"Are *you* afraid?" asked GungGung.

I wanted to tell him I was scared out of my mind! But I couldn't. How could I say that I was freaked out by dead bodies and ghosts when GungGung was afraid of something completely different?

"As for dying," said GungGung, "I was more afraid of it when I was younger. But now I've got friends on the other side."

"You mean Charlie?" I asked.

"Charlie, and my mom and dad," said Gung-

Gung. "My grandparents too, and a bunch of aunts and uncles, a cousin, and several other good friends."

"Oh," I said. I thought about it. I pictured all these people waving to GungGung from the other side of Walden Pond. But swimming all the way to the other side is creepy. The water gets really dark and cold in the middle, and you could drown before you get there.

"What if there's no other side?" I asked. "What if when you die, it's over? That's it. You're finished. There's nothing more."

"Would I be afraid to die then?" asked Gung-Gung.

I nodded.

GungGung looked at me in that way that my mom does when she wants to see to the bottom of me. He took a big breath.

"If there's absolutely nothing after this life?" asked GungGung. "Then I wouldn't be afraid of death at all—how could you be afraid of nothing? But I would be terribly afraid of not having really lived while I had the chance."

"Oh?" I said.

"But there's a way to avoid that," said Gung-Gung.

"How?" I asked.

"Make a bucket list," said GungGung.

"A bucket list?" I asked. "What's a bucket list?"

"It's a list of all the things you want to do before you die," said GungGung.

Yikes!

"I've actually been thinking a lot about this since Charlie died," said GungGung. "But Poh-Poh, being old-fashioned Chinese, wouldn't let me do it, she thought it would bring me bad luck."

"What kind of bad luck?" I asked.

"The worst kind," whispered GungGung. "Death."

I snorted milk up my nose.

"You gotta look death smack in the eye, son," said GungGung. "Otherwise, you'll miss out on life."

"Look 'im smack in the eye?" I asked. I didn't like looking anyone in the eye.

"You ought to make a bucket list too," said GungGung. "If I had made one at your age, I would have done a lot of spectacular things by now."

GungGung got up and handed me a pen and a piece of paper.

"Get in touch with your inner old guy," said GungGung. "He'll show you a few things about yourself."

"My inner old guy?"

"Your bucket list will reveal what's really important to you," he said.

Then GungGung took a pen and a piece of paper, and this is what he wrote:

My Bucket List

1. Spend more time with grandkids.
2. Take grandkids to a Red Sox game.
3. Take grandkids to a dragon boat race.
4. Tell PohPoh how much I love her every day.
5. Bring PohPoh more flowers.
6. Write the story of my life.

7. See the Serengeti.
8. Climb Mt. Kilimanjaro (with my eyes).
9. Learn Spanish.
10. Sleep more.
11. Exercise less.
12. Play more mah-jongg.
13. Learn to dance.
14. Dance at Calvin's, Alvin's and Anibelly's weddings.

"DANCE AT MY WEDDING???!!!" I cried. "I'M NOT GETTING MARRIED UNLESS IT'S TO MY HAMSTER!!!"

"Fine," said GungGung.

"But I don't have a hamster," I said.

So GungGung crossed off number fourteen.

14. ~~Dance at Calvin, Alvin and Anibelly's weddings.~~

Then GungGung sat back with his list. He looked very pleased.

But I was not.

There had been death omens all week, but a bucket list was definitely the creepiest one of all!

"That's as far as I'll go," said GungGung, rereading his list and chuckling to himself. "Some people have a hundred things on their list, but I haven't got that much time left."

Not that much time left? It was just as I'd suspected!

"You and your siblings are at the very top of my list," said GungGung, giving me a friendly slap on the back. "I hope you know how important you are to me."

I wanted to give him a friendly slap back. But I couldn't. My hands were stuck down at my sides, useless, like a couple of oars frozen to the sides of a boat.

"How's your list?" asked GungGung.

My list was blank.

There wasn't even a bucket on it.

What did a bucket have to do with it anyway?

But I learned something about myself . . .

I didn't know where my inner old guy was.

But I'm super-duper old-fashioned Chinese, that's for sure.

CHAPTER THIRTEEN

The Nail in the Coffin

it wasn't long before GungGung went to take a nap on the sofa in our living room, and I hurried upstairs with his bucket list to show Calvin and Anibelly.

"Look, Cal—" I started to say, running into my room.

But before another syllable came out of my mouth, something that felt like a house sailing out of the clear blue sky landed on top of me, flattening me against the floor.

Oooommmmpf. My toes pointed downwards.

It was a house named Calvin.

"I can't believe you let that happen!" cried Calvin, squeezing me between his knees. "Thou burly-boned, mad-brained malt worm!"

"It wasn't my fault!" I cried.

"Thou pukey, lumpish idle-headed hugger-mugger!" said Calvin.

"But I can't talk in school," I wailed.

"You can shake your head," said Calvin. "You can write. . . . You can gesture. . . .

"You can talk with your eyes," he added. "You're not exactly dead, you know."

"But I'm—cough—nearly dead now!" I squeaked. "Help! Anibelly, help me!"

But Anibelly only stared, her mouth opened in an O. Watching me get killed by Calvin is the second-best spectator sport around our house, next to watching me get busted by my dad.

So Calvin sat harder.

Milk sprayed out of my nose.

"GungGung!" Anibelly cried excitedly. "Come quick! Come quick! Alvin's getting killed! Alvin's getting killed!"

"Owwwwooooooo," howled Lucy.

I pounded on the floor with my fists. But I knew that downstairs GungGung was in Stage Three deep sleep with no eye movement or muscle activity and there was no way that he would hear the ruckus and come save my tuckus.

"Owwwwwwww!" I cried. *"Owwwwwwww!"*

Calvin sat even harder.

Then I went limp. Like a squirrel flattened out by the side of the road. This made Calvin twitch and lift just a little and I slipped out from under him, like a snake from under a rock. This always works; even though Calvin's a killing machine, sitting on roadkill makes him squirm.

I gulped the air hungrily and noisily.

Then I looked at Calvin. He had turned a purpley plum from being super-duper mad at me, and his eyes were still puffy and red like they were in school. But lucky for me, he wasn't in a killing mood anymore.

"How did you think I felt when the principal called me into her office and said she was very sorry that my grandpa had died?" asked Calvin. "And how did you think I felt when the next thing I knew, I was invited to his memorial service with your second-grade class?"

Calvin wiped his eyes and nose on his sleeve. Calvin rarely cries, but when he does, he doesn't recover very quickly.

"I'm a *fourth grader*, you know," said Calvin.

"Don't be mad, Cal," I said. "GungGung *is* going to die. Look!"

I held out the paper.

"GungGung made his BUCKET LIST!" I screeched, holding out the piece of paper.

"What's a bucket list?" asked Anibelly.

"It's like a Last Will and Testament," I said. "You write it before you die—but instead of saying who gets your stuff, you say what you want to do before you go for your final bus ride!"

"Then what?" asked Anibelly.

"Then you do it," I said. "And then you die!"

"Lemme see that," said Calvin, taking the paper from me.

Calvin read it silently.

Then he read it again.

"What does it say?" asked Anibelly.

"It says he wants to spend a lot of time with us," said Calvin.

"That's what he said." I nodded.

"This is serious," said Calvin.

"IT'S THE NAIL IN THE COFFIN!!!" I shrieked.

"Hmmm," said Calvin. "But look, number six says he wants to write his life's story."

"So?"

"He's not a very good writer," said Calvin. "It takes him forever to write anything. Then he goes back and changes everything. He'll be at it until we're as old as he is now."

Calvin looked really relieved.

Then he put his arm around me.

"It's really scary thinking about GungGung dying," said Calvin.

I nodded.

"But it makes me more sad than scared," said Calvin.

"Me too," said Anibelly.

I thought about it.

Calvin and Anibelly were right. When GungGung dies, it'll be so sad that the moon will cry.

And that's very different from being scared.

"If I were you," said Calvin, "I'd be freaked out about going to Charlie's funeral, not about GungGung dying."

Silence.

"Do you have any idea how creepy a dead body is?" asked Calvin.

Silence.

Calvin hurried to the computer.

Click, click, click, went Calvin's finger on the mouse.

"Did you know that they *embalm* your body when you die?" asked Calvin.

"What's that?" I asked. But I really didn't want to know.

"It's modern mummification," said Calvin. "It's so you can look good at your funeral. First they clean your body with a strong disinfectant, then they replace all your blood with embalming fluid to keep you from rotting."

I was really sorry I asked.

"But if you're Tibetan, they won't do that to you," said Calvin. "In Tibet they do sky burials— leaving your body at the top of a mountain for the vultures to eat."

Gulp!

"In Africa, you could get buried under or next to your house," Calvin continued. "And they'll bury you with your eating utensils, walking sticks, blankets and other useful items that you'll need in your next life."

"Let's move to Africa," I said. "You can put me behind the garage."

"In India, they'll cremate you within twenty-four hours," said Calvin.

Silence.

I didn't ask. I didn't want to know.

Calvin scrolled down the page.

"Did you know that typically a dead body cools about one degree a minute until it reaches room temperature?" asked Calvin.

I closed my ears. I didn't want to hear any more. I was getting closer and closer by the minute to that creepy funeral.

"Aaaaaaaaaaaaaaaaaaaaaaaaaack!" I screamed. *"Aaaaaaaaaaaaaaaaack!"*

Then I ran downstairs and out into the yard.

Outside, the air was already beginning to smell like moonlight. I charged full speed ahead, screaming at the top of my lungs. *"AAAAAAAAAAAAAAAAAAAAAAAAAAAACK!"*

Then I stepped back. In the half-sunlight, half-moonlight just before the sky turns inky dark, our house glowed from every window.

And the moon hovered like a giant white pearl above our chimney. It meant that my mom would soon be home from work. And my dad too.

Normally, I love seeing the moon above our house. But there was something not quite normal about the moon tonight— what was that? It looked like two twiggy insects on our roof, their black wiry arms gesturing like crazy against the silvery moon.

"Hey, Sport!" one of them called out, waving at me.

"Uncle Dennis?"

"I came over to give your dad a hand," said Uncle Dennis. "You were so busy that I didn't get a chance to say hi!"

"Dad?"

"Hey, son," said the other figure.

"What are you doing up there?" I asked.

"I came home early to start on the roof," said my dad, perched like a mantis against the moon. "It's a big job and it needs to be done before winter."

I froze.

Suddenly, Mr. Arlecchino's voice filled my ears. "Roofing isn't a hobby—it's a dangerous job. . . . One twist of the ankle and it's Do-It-Yourself Ho no more."

I couldn't breathe.

I couldn't blink.

I couldn't move.

Were those death omens not meant for GungGung after all—but for—gasp!—UNCLE DENNIS and MY DAD???

Did I have the nail in the wrong coffin this whole time?

Everything began to spin around me—the trees, our house, our driveway, all my carved sticks, Louise, my dad, Uncle Dennis, nails and hammers, roof tiles, toads, worms, crickets, everything.

"*AAAAAAAAAAAAAAAAAAAACK!!!*"
I screamed. "*AAAAAAAAAAAAAAACK!!!*"

It was the last thing I heard. But I was sure nothing came out of my mouth.

Worse, it'd been a LONG time since I'd used the bathroom.

CHAPTER FOURTEEN

Relieved

poor me.

This is what you do after you've had one of *those* accidents.

You crawl into bed.

You curl into a little ball.

You die.

"Waaaaaaaaaaah!" I cried.
"Waaaaaaaaaaaaaah!"

Finally, my dad came in to read to us, like he does every night before bed. Tonight we got to the part where Odysseus escapes the Cyclops, Polyphemus, by blinding him with a steak.

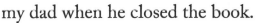

"Sounds like you've had a rougher day than Odysseus," said my dad when he closed the book.

I nodded. I was sitting very close to my dad, leaning against him to hold him up, like I do every night on account of he's at that age where he needs all the help he can get. Calvin and Anibelly were holding him up from the other side.

"Do you have something to tell me, son?" my dad asked.

I love it when he calls me that. Son. I love it more than my own name. I love it so much that hearing it could make me cry. So I did. *"Waaaaaaaaaaaaaaaaaaaaaaaah!"*

Then all my troubles came pouring out, from my toenails, past my gut, up my chest, out of my mouth and into my dad's ears.

I breathed in.

I breathed out.

My dad said nothing. He put his book down. He put one arm around Calvin and Anibelly and his other arm around me and pulled me so close everything disappeared. I breathed in. I breathed out. I love the smell of my dad.

Then I really cried. "*WAAAAAAAAAAAAH!*" I cried so hard I couldn't stop.

Finally, when I had to take a time-out, I told my dad to keep holding me, I never wanted him to let go, ever. So he didn't. He said he would hold me forever if that was what I wanted him to do.

"How 'bout when you're dead?" I asked. "You won't be able to hold me then."

"That's true," said my dad.

"You could fall off that roof tomorrow and be dead," I said.

"True," said my dad.

"Then why are you doing it, Dad?" I asked. "One twist of the ankle and you're history!"

"I like taking care of my things," said my dad. "And that includes working on our house and making everything safe and comfortable for my family."

"But it's not safe for you, Dad," I said. "Or for Uncle Dennis."

"I'm really sorry I've alarmed you," said my dad. "But your uncle Dennis and I are extremely careful and taking every precaution. We don't want to be history either."

I could feel Anibelly and Calvin squeezing closer to my dad on the other side.

"Aren't you afraid of dying, Dad?" asked Calvin. "And leaving us as half orphans?"

"And mom as a widow spider?" I added.

"Every day," said my dad. "I'm afraid of it every day."

My dad gave us a long squeeze.

"Before I became a dad, I wasn't afraid of dying," he said. "I did daredevil stunts with your uncle Dennis that should have killed us both. It's a miracle we survived to our ripe old ages. I wouldn't even think of doing any of those things today."

"Why not?" asked Calvin. "Does being a dad make you a wimp?"

"Not at all," said my dad. "Being a dad is the bravest thing a man can do. But it also makes him more afraid than ever of injury and death."

"How can you be bravest and afraidest?" asked Anibelly.

"Because I don't want to miss a day of your lives," said my dad.

"Dad?" I said.

"Yes?"

"What if there's something that's extremely dangerous and super-duper creepy, would you do it?" I asked.

"Hmmm," said my dad, looking at me sideways. "You don't mean something like . . . going to a funeral, do you?"

I nodded.

"Saying goodbye to someone we love is very important," said my dad. "But I can understand your fright, son, and if you'd really rather not go, then you need to tell GungGung."

"You mean I don't have to go?" I asked.

"You don't have to go," said my dad.

"Wouldn't GungGung miss me?" I asked.

"I'm sure he would," said my dad. "But you need to be honest with him. He'll understand if you're not ready."

I nodded.

I wanted to be ready, but I wasn't.

"I made a promise that was bigger than I was," I said, shamefully.

"You meant well," said my dad.

My dad leaned in and kissed the top of my head. I love it when he does that.

"Maybe you're actually bigger than your promise," said my dad. "You just don't know it yet."

It was a good word from my dad. He knew that I knew that he knew that sometimes a good word from him changes everything.

But this time it changed nothing.

I was more freaked out about Charlie's funeral than ever.

And I was relieved to know that I didn't have to go.

CHAPTER FIFTEEN

How to Pass a History Test

this is how to pass a history test.

Plan A:

1. On the school bus, try to remember some historical stuff.

2. If you can't remember any old stuff, don't panic.

3. Go to Plan B.

Plan B:

1. Look like you are paying attention.
2. Do not wear a mask.

3. Do not wear garlic.

4. Go to Plan C.

Plan C:

1. When Miss P talks about Algonkians and Puritans, it's a secret code of some sort.

2. Crack the code.

3. If you haven't cracked the code by the time she's passing out the test, there's only one thing left to do.

4. Go to Plan D.

Plan D:

D is not a good name for a plan.
Go to Plan F.

Plan F:

F is not a good name for a plan either.
Go to Plan G.

Plan G:

1. G is a very Good letter for a plan.
2. When you get the test, look at it.
3. Look around.
4. Try to PASS your test to someone.
5. If you fail at #4, go to #6.
6. Keep your hands in plain sight.
7. Lift the paper to your mouth.
8. Open mouth.
9. Insert.
10. Chew slowly and carefully.
11. Pretend it's pizza. It will help.

Calvin didn't say anything about
it being very dry or the girl sitting next to me
whose one good eye was fixed on me, unblinking.

"Eeeeuuuw!" said Flea. She was supposed to
be looking at her own test, but she was not. Her
eye was as round as a magnifying glass.

"Miss P, ALVIN'S EATING HIS TEST!"
cried Flea.

All heads turned.

All eyes were on my test.

"Oh, Alvin," said Miss P. "You poor thing."

I drooled.

"You've been through so much this week," said Miss P, "I should have asked if you wanted to take your test next week."

Gulp.

It tasted terrible.

Worse, Miss P sent me to the nurse's office.

And the nurse called my mom to take me home.

"Alvin," said my mom when she came to pick me up. "Tomorrow will be better."

I didn't think so.

I was miserable.

I didn't nod.

I didn't smile.

I didn't even look at my mom.

I hung my head.

And clutched my stomach.

And I went home.

And it wasn't even lunchtime yet.

CHAPTER SIXTEEN

Here Lies the Body of Alvin Ho

a friday afternoon at home was heaven.

The light was bright.

The sky was blue.

Cotton-candy clouds floated past.

After making a bunch of holes in my yard, and running around a bit with Lucy, I was flat on my back in a ditch of my own digging, marveling at my good luck. I'd never intended to come home early, I had only intended to pass my history test. But a free afternoon at home was as good as playing hooky, without the worry of getting busted.

The afternoon would have been perfect except for one thing.

Anibelly.

"Lalalalalalalala," sang Anibelly, digging a hole nearby. "Lalalalalalalalala."

I wished my mom had left her at day care, but she hadn't. My mom said that she would work from home this afternoon while I convalesced, whatever that is, and there was no sense in leaving Anibelly at Little Ducklings Daycare.

"You wanna be buried?" asked Anibelly, her head suddenly floating like a volleyball above mine. She smiled.

"You mean like at the beach?" I asked.

"Yup," said Anibelly. "It might feel good."

"Okay," I said. "Dirt always feels good."

"Yup," said Anibelly. She picked up a shovel.

Dirt flew.

Rocks rolled.

Worms wiggled past my head.

"Jingle bells, jingle bells, jingle all the way," sang Anibelly in rhythm with her shovel. *"Oh what fun it is to ride in a one-horse open sleigh, hey!"*

I closed my eyes.

Anibelly's favorite song is "Jingle Bells" and she sings it whenever she's in a good mood.

"Jingle bells, jingle bells, jingle all the way!" Anibelly blasted like a rock star. Shovel, shovel. Pat, pat.

I kept my eyes closed.

I lay as still as the dead.

"Do you like the singing?" Anibelly asked.

"I like it very much," I said. "Jingle Bells" is my favorite too.

Shovel, shovel.

Pat, pat.

"How does it feel?" asked Anibelly.

The earth was cool against my chest.

My face was wet with Lucy kisses.

My butt was cold.

My fingers dug deeper into the soft dirt.

"I like it," I said. "It's very peaceful."

I wondered if Charlie was going to feel the

same way when they buried him tomorrow. And I wondered if he'd hear the same things:

Birds singing.

A squirrel hurrying up a tree.

The breath of someone nearby.

I smelled the sunlight.

"It's like I'm at the beach," I said. "But better."

"Would you like me to say some nice words about you?" asked Anibelly.

"Yes, please," I said.

"Okay," said Anibelly.

She let go of the shovel. *Bonk!*

She waved her hands toward the sky.

"Oh, God," said Anibelly, closing her eyes. "Here lies the body of Alvin Ho. Aged seven. No cell phone number. No cell phone."

Silence.

"Is that all?" I asked.

"You want more?" asked Anibelly.

"They fit a whole book on those tombstones," I said.

"You want a tombstone?" asked Anibelly.

"No," I said. "I just want to hear the nice words."

Anibelly took a big breath. "Once upon a time he was afraid of everything," she began.

I closed my eyes and listened.

"He shared . . . but not always. He got busted a lot. He cried all the time. He could scream his head off. He played with Lucy. He loved his mom and dad. He was the best Firecracker Man ever. Rest in pieces. The end."

"Do you have any holy water?" I asked. "And incense?"

"You want the fancy stuff?"

"I want the works," I said. "Like on TV."

"Okay!" said Anibelly. She hurried into the . house.

When she ran back out, she was carrying her art case, but it was now marked "FⅭK."

"What's FⅭK?" I asked.

"Funeral Disaster Kit," said Anibelly. "I made it for you when you told Gung-Gung you would go with him."

"You did?"

"Yup," said Anibelly. "I knew you were scared."

"Oh," I said.

"Now that you're not going," said Anibelly, "we can use it for your own funeral."

"What's in it?" I asked.

"Something that makes it okay to be scared," said Anibelly, opening the case and pulling out a rag that was limp and kind of dirty.

"What is it?" I asked.

"My blankie," said Anibelly. "I cut it in half."

"You cut your blankie???" I was shocked. It was the best thing she owned.

"You were so scared," said Anibelly. She squatted down and rubbed it on my cheek.

"Half for you and half for me," she said, leaving the soft, fuzzy, chewed and tattered cloth next to my cheek.

I inhaled.

It smelled like Anibelly. She smelled like half-baby, half-alien.

"Half is all you need," said Anibelly. "Just rub it between your fingers, like this."

Anibelly rubbed the corner like a lucky penny.

"It's a secret weapon," she whispered.

I didn't know what to say.

What do you say when someone's just given you the best secret weapon in the world?

Then Anibelly pulled out my mom's plastic bottle of holy water, the one with the spray nozzle, and misted my entire head.

"That's for just in case," she said. "Amen."

Then Anibelly went back to digging holes.

"Lalalalalalala," she sang. "Lalalalalalala."

And I went back to watching the brilliant sky, my cheek rubbing on her half blankie. I thought about what it must feel like to be dead and to spend every afternoon with nothing to do but blink away rainbow tears on my eyelashes.

It was fantastic. It was really fantastic.

CHAPTER SEVENTEEN

How to Dress for a Funeral

this is how to dress for a funeral:

1. Clean shirt.
2. Clean pants.
3. Clean jacket.
4. Clip-on tie.
5. Clean underwear.
6. If you forget the clean underwear, take everything off and redo steps one through four.
7. Clean socks.
8. Clean shoes.

9. Half-blankie in the pocket.

10. Holy water and garlic in the other pocket, just in case.

No one had to tell me. I'd figured it out all by myself.

It was no problem either.

The only problem was that every time I dress like this, something terrible happens. Like the time I tripped over some wires while dancing at my aunt Sushi's wedding and everything went dark. Or the time I went to my baby cousin's christening and all the aunties pinched my cheeks and kissed them. After that, I choked on jellyfish and had to be rushed to the emergency room.

The suit was a magnet for bad luck or something, I was sure of it.

•●•●•

Downstairs my mom and dad were sitting in the kitchen reading the paper and drinking coffee. Anibelly and Calvin were in the living room watching Saturday-morning cartoons.

Normally, I'd be watching cartoons too.

But I was not normal.

I was going to my first funeral.

"Oh, Alvin!" My mom gasped when I came down the stairs.

Stomp. Stomp. Stomp. I stepped stiffly; it was another problem with the suit.

"You look so handsome and brave!" cried my mom.

"Amazing," said my dad. "You really surprise me sometimes, son. I didn't think that you were up for this."

"I. Didn't. Think. I. Was. Up. For. It. Either." A strange little voice came out of my mouth. I sat down and reached for my mom's yummy homemade granola.

"What changed your mind?" asked my dad.

"I thought about it for a long time yesterday while I was

dead," I squeaked. Milk and nuts dribbled off my chin.

Then my dad added, "I'm very proud of you, son."

I was proud of me too, but I was also scared out of my mind. My mouth opened, and all that came out was—

Ding-dong!

My heart jumped out of my chest.

I ran to the door. GungGung and PohPoh were coming to pick me up, but it wasn't them.

It was Flea.

"Hi!" said Flea. She's a girl and she was all dressed up like a girl too, which, as everyone knows, is horrible, especially when it makes her look clean and shiny like a new car.

"What are you doing here?" I asked.

"I came to go to the funeral with you," she said.

"You did?"

"Yup," she said.

"Why?"

"Well, I'm your desk buddy, aren't I?" asked Flea.

I nodded.

"I sit with you on the bus, don't I?" she asked.

I nodded again.

"If your gunggung had died, I would be going, wouldn't I?" Her one good eye blinked.

"No," I said.

"Of course I would," said Flea. "I don't have a grandpa. But if I could order one on the Internet, I'd click on yours."

"Oh," I said. I didn't know that about Flea.

"I'm just SO happy it's NOT your gunggung," said Flea, stepping past me and going straight into my house like she always does. "But I think that you still need a funeral buddy."

A funeral buddy?

Like I said, my suit attracts all sorts of bad luck, especially the girl kind.

•◦•◦•

It was a bright, cold morning, with a little breeze and little puffs of clouds in the sky; a good-luck day for a funeral, GungGung said. He and PohPoh were very pleased that Flea had joined us, and after struggling to get my stiff body into their car, we drove to the funeral home, where they struggled again to take my stiff body out of the car.

Then we went inside.

It was *so* creepy.

I would have fainted dead away if it hadn't been for Flea, who was really experienced at these sorts of things.

First she smelled the flowers.

So I smelled the flowers.

Then she shook the hands of everyone Poh-Poh and GungGung introduced to us.

"This is our friend, Sophie," said my gunggung. "And this is our grandson, Alvin. He knew Charlie too."

I shook stiffly.

I stared straight ahead.

Then, out of the corner of my eye, I saw it.

The *dead body*.

It looked like Charlie. Sort of.

A strange, sad feeling went up my nose and fell into my chest.

I thought about the times when he looked like normal Charlie.

I reached into my pocket and rubbed Anibelly's half-blankie between my fingers.

I watched as people walked up to the casket and bowed three times.

"It's a Chinese thing," whispered Gung-Gung. "It shows respect. You do it if you want to, it's not required."

Then he and PohPoh did it together.

Then Flea did it. And she didn't even know him!

No way was I doing that.

Stomp. Stomp. Stomp.

I couldn't believe it. I was marching closer and closer to the casket!

My feet stopped right in front of Charlie. Yikes!

Bow. Bow. Bow.

Turn.

Stomp. Stomp. Stomp.

I wanted to run out of that place as fast as I could. But I couldn't. Instead, I marched over to where my gunggung and Poh-Poh and Flea were sitting, waiting for the service to begin.

I sat down stiffly. My heart pounded like crazy.

"You made Charlie proud," said my gung-gung, giving me a pat on the back. "But I'm even prouder."

PohPoh put one arm around me and the other arm around Flea and said something in Chinese that sounded like we were very, very brave.

If she only knew.

Then GungGung got up. He made a speech about Charlie, reading it from a piece of paper that shook in his hands:

"He was a great guy. . . .

"He was always there for me. . . .

"We grew up in China. . . .

"My family was poor, so he shared his rice with me. . . .

"During the war, he hid me in caves. . . .

"When I was scared, he told me stories. . . .

"When I was cold, he shared his blanket. . . .

"He was like a brother to me. . . .

"He was poor like me, but I never knew it. . . .

"I thought he owned all of China. . . ."

GungGung wiped his eyes and blew his nose at the end of his speech. And so did everyone else.

And so did I. I cried into Anibelly's half-blankie, then rubbed it on my cheek.

•◦•◦•

"Alvin?" said a voice. "Are you okay, son?"

I blinked.

It was my dad. He was in his roofing gear.

"Where am I?" I asked, sitting up.

"You fell asleep in the car on the way home," said my dad. "And GungGung carried you in."

I looked around. I was on the sofa in my living room.

Then I remembered. I looked around for Flea. Fortunately, there was no sign of her.

"How was the funeral?" asked my mom.

"Creepy," I said. "I was scared the whole time."

"Sounds like you did okay," said my dad. "GungGung said you were on your best behavior. And that you and Flea enjoyed the Chinese banquet afterwards."

"Yup," I said. "But I enjoyed the Concord Museum even more."

"Concord Museum?" asked my mom. "GungGung didn't mention that."

"Everyone knows you can't go directly home after a funeral," I said. "Just in case."

"In case of what?" asked my dad.

"In case there are bad spirits following you," I explained. "PohPoh said that you gotta dodge them somewhere."

"The museum's the perfect place to take them," said my mom. "They should feel right at home among all the historical stuff."

I nodded. "It was the perfect place to take me too," I said. "There was an entire room about the Algonkians and Puritans."

"I'd forgotten," said my dad.

"It really helps to see everything," I said.

"Does this mean you'll be ready to take your test again next week?" asked my mom.

"Take it again?" I asked. "Why do I have to do that?"

"Well, you didn't take it in the first place," said my mom. "You still have to pass it."

"Pass it?" I squeaked. "But Calvin said all I had to do was eat it."

Alvin Ho's
Deadly Glossary

afterlife— Aka "the other side," which is the other side of Walden Pond, which is where you end up after you swim for your life across the pond.

Algonkian— Pronounced "al-GON-kee-un." I think the Algonkians beat Calvin's team, the Patriots, in baseball. Also it's a word like "American" or "Asian" that refers to a lot of different people. Algonkians include many Native American tribes that live throughout the United States and southern Canada. The tribes have different names and cultures, but their native languages were related.

American Revolutionary War— Started in Concord, Massachusetts, which is hard to spell. Fought between the Revolutionaries (the good guys) and the Redcoats (the British Army). It lasted a long time, from 1775 to 1783. There were dead bodies all over the place. Nowadays, they try to restart the war every April, on Patriots' Day!

Ben Franklin— Was a very busy dude. He did everything: wrote books, printed a newspaper, invented stuff, played several musical instruments, composed music, wrote lots of letters (and sent them too on account of he was the boss at the U.S. Post Office) and helped write the Declaration of Independence. Most importantly, he experimented with electricity and invented the lightning rod!

bucket list— Stuff you want to do before you die. It's a list, but it has nothing to do with a bucket, that's for sure.

condolence letter— Something you write to someone when you're about to die.

cremate— I didn't ask. I didn't want to know. But it sounds like it has something to do with turning you into cream.

Egyptian Pyramids— Built as tombs for the dead bodies of kings and queens. Constructed before the Flood. Noah and his animals probably saw the tops of them as they floated by in the ark.

Fenway Green— The color of split-pea soup. Made only for Fenway Park. You can't get it anywhere, but you can mix your own and come pretty close, like my gunggung did.

Fenway Park— Opened on April 20, 1912, the day after Patriots' Day, and less than a week after the *Titanic* sank. Gulp.

Firecracker Man— Saves the world on Saturdays and holidays.

funeral— Creepy ceremony for saying goodbye to someone when they die. Usually includes a dead body.

Great Wall of China— More than 4,000 miles long. While it was being constructed, people called it the longest cemetery on earth on account of workers who died got buried in it. More than one million people died building the wall.

Green Monster— The big green wall in left field at Fenway Park where the balls bang off like crazy! The old-fashioned scoreboard is at the bottom of the wall. This means there's an old-fashioned person inside the wall who takes the old number off and puts the new number up every time a team scores. That's a job I'd like to have!

GungGung— (1) Married to PohPoh. (2) My grandpa from my mom's side. (3) An ace pitching machine. (4) A ~~die-hard~~ loyal Red Sox fan. (5) My best friend next to my dad.

HBP— Hit By Pitch. Don "No-Rub" Baylor got hit 267 times! It's the record. He played for the Red Sox back in the desktop age before batteries were invented for laptops.

Henry David Thoreau— Born in Concord, just like me, and died here too. Gulp. He spent his life trying to know what it meant to be truly alive. He died when he was 44.

Homer— (1) Famous dead poet who wrote the Lily Ad and the Odd Sea, true tales of indomitable courage and dangerous expeditions. (2) Lived in Greece while the continents were still drifting. (3) Never lived in Concord. (4) Some say he never lived at all and that his poems were written by someone with the same name. (5) Blind. (6) Probably homeless. (7) Wore a toga.

Leif Eriksson— Brave Viking explorer who was the first European to go camping in North America.

Lobsterbacks— Aka Redcoats. Their uniforms made them look like genuine Maine lobsters!

Louisa May Alcott— Creepy dead author who's still leading tours through her home. Wrote a book called *Little Women* that sold like crazy and still sells like crazy. It's crazy—it's about girls!

Lotus Eaters— People who eat lotus, which is a flower with a yummy fruit. After you eat it, all you want to do is sleep and then eat some more. This is a problem when you're supposed to be having adventures and heading home from a war, like Odysseus's men.

Minutemen— A small, hand-picked elite force of the Massachusetts militia, who were "ready in a minute." They were the first to arrive at a battle during the American Revolutionary War. On April 19, 1775, they came to Concord on foot. Nowadays, some of the troops ride the bus.

Moong cha cha— Chinese words for confused, fuzzy in the head, not clear.

Mumbo jumbo— Spelling, math, history, girls. Anything that looks confusing, sounds confusing and will never make any sense no matter how loud you scream.

Nail in the coffin— Used to keep the lid from falling off. Especially helpful for keeping scary vampires inside, I think.

Nathaniel Hawthorne— Famous dead author who lived next door to the Alcotts on Lexington Road. Rarely gives house tours, not like the other famous dead authors in town.

Odysseus— (1) The original action hero, star of Homer's Odd Sea. (2) A Greek dude. (3) Fought a long war against the Trojans, who were bigger and better. (4) Came up with the idea of hiding Greek soldiers inside a wooden horse and conquering the Trojans by surprise. (5) Very brave, but was allergic to flying, so it took him ten years to get home after the war. (6) The good news is that he had a lot of dangerous adventures on the way!

Omen— A creepy message that's not written in words, but first you have to figure out it's a message, then you have to figure out what it means. Then you run!

Pangaea— (1) Pottery shards floating in black car oil in our garage. (2) The name of the landmass that separated into different continents.

PohPoh— (1) Married to GungGung. (2) My mom's mom. (3) My granny. (4) Oh, how I love her!

Puritans— Not as good as the Patriots (Calvin's team), and much worse than the Algonkians (Little League champs).

Ralph Waldo Emerson— Famous dead author who hired Henry David Thoreau to mow his lawn, babysit his kids, and fix stuff around his house.

Red Sox— Everyone knows who they are—the best team in the world!

Shakespeare— English dude who wrote so many plays and poems that some say he didn't write them at all, but that his works were written by Bacon or Oxford. I didn't know bacon could write! That's fantastic!

Trojan War— The greatest war in Greek mythology, fought between the Greeks and the Trojans. See Odysseus.

Tuojiangosaurus— A punk-looking vegetarian dinosaur that lived in southern China in the Late Jurassic Period. His name means "Tuo River Lizard."

Wasabi— Japanese horseradish paste. Looks like paste. Feels like paste. Smells like paste. But it's not like the paste you eat in school. It will blow your head off and make you cry!

In addition to writing the popular Alvin Ho series, **LENORE LOOK** is the author of the Ruby Lu series. She has also written several acclaimed picture books, including *Henry's First-Moon Birthday, Uncle Peter's Amazing Chinese Wedding,* and *Polka Dot Penguin Pottery.* Lenore lives in Randolph, New Jersey.

As well as creating the art for the acclaimed Alvin Ho series, **LEUYEN PHAM** is the illustrator of Jennifer LaRue Huget's *The Best Birthday Party Ever;* Kelly DiPucchio's *Grace for President,* a *New York Times* bestseller; and Julianne Moore's Freckleface Strawberry series. She is the author and illustrator of *Big Sister, Little Sister.* LeUyen lives in San Francisco. Learn more at leuyenpham.com.

Afraid you've missed one of the Alvin Ho books?
Fear no more!

Alvin Ho: Allergic to Girls, School, and Other Scary Things

Alvin Ho: Allergic to Camping, Hiking, and Other Natural Disasters

Alvin Ho: Allergic to Birthday Parties, Science Projects, and Other Man-Made Catastrophes

Alvin Ho: Allergic to Dead Bodies, Funerals, and Other Fatal Circumstances